# FROM BENEATH THE ASHES

## Brian S. Marro

## iUniverse, Inc.
New York  Lincoln  Shanghai

# FROM BENEATH THE ASHES

iUniverse, Inc.

For information address:
iUniverse, Inc.
2021 Pine Lake Road, Suite 100
Lincoln, NE 68512
www.iuniverse.com

ISBN: 0-595-30527-X

Printed in the United States of America

# Contents

▼

# THE INTRODUCTION

It was cold and rainy in Rockville Centre, Long Island, on November 27th in the year 1959. That morning, in Mercy Hospital, Beth Larson was giving birth to her first son, a six-pound, fourteen-ounce bouncing baby boy. Named after his grandfather, he was pronounced as Henry Edward Larson. Henry's father, Richard, was a quiet, soft-spoken man who always preached the importance of hard work and strict family values. Richard was an only child who spent most of his life as a CPA in a large, prestigious New York accounting firm. He worked long hours and many weekends to provide a living for his family that he did not experience while growing up. Beth, who was the stronger, more dominant parent, had come from the Midwest and was old school. She stayed home as a full-time mother in their Valley Stream, Long Island home with Henry's older sister Susan, and eventually, his little brother Glen. Valley Stream was just over the Queen's border into Long Island. It was considered an average suburban neighborhood in middle-class America.

In school, Henry was one of those nerdy types that bigger kids constantly enjoyed picking on. You know the type—quiet, glasses, and meticulously well dressed. Sometimes acting as a "know-it-all," showing up the wrong kids in class. As a result, sometimes they would take his lunch money while at other times they just enjoyed beating up on him. Henry endured this through grammar school, and it continued until he graduated from high school in 1977. Although his grades in school were only a little better than average, he excelled in finding ways to get other students to do his work for him. As he was exceptional in math, he would often trade math work with students who suffered in that area. In return, they would do his science or history projects. This was a great trade-off for Henry. Math came to him easy, and often he would finish the other kids' homework in a matter of minutes, while they, in turn, spent hours on those "boring" tedious science and history reports. Of course sometimes he allowed his class-mates to copy from him during a big test, but that always cost them more: either lunch money or some other project Henry didn't want to do. Even as a youth, Henry felt that he was above his peers, and he enjoyed manipulating them in these areas.

After graduating from Valley Stream High School, Henry spent two years at Nassau County Community College—a local junior college in Hempstead, Long Island—before transferring to St. John's University, where he graduated with a degree in business. While at St. John's, he met his bride-to-be: Kate Falcone.

Kate Falcone, like Henry, was very reserved. Kate was also an only child, with very little family background. She had moved to New York from Bethlehem, Pennsylvania, just before attending St. John's. Kate was a big-boned woman, bigger than Henry, but quite a devoted and loving person. Kate's parents had her late in life and both had passed early in hers. She grew up with her Aunt Ellen and left home for college, never to return.

Henry and Kate were both business majors who shared several classes together. For Henry, it was his first and only serious relationship in college. He dated very infrequently, and most college girls wouldn't even look his way, but he and Kate were a good match. They were both very intelligent and neither very attractive. They found themselves always together, doing projects or papers for their mutual classes. By their senior year they were inseparable. Both Henry and Kate graduated in the summer of 1981 and married less than a year later.

They went through the usual struggles young couples endure. Henry moved from job to job, trying to find something that was "challenging enough" for him. His first two jobs—one as a clerk in Metropolitan Life, the other as an assistant office manager for Travelers Insurance—provided very little satisfaction, either professionally or financially. Henry felt that he was destined for much bigger and better things. During his short tenure at these jobs he would belittle his co-work-ers, eventually wearing out his welcome. In 1986 he took a job for Bevel Bressler, a downtown brokerage firm on Wall Street. Impressed by his interview, the company put Henry through their training program. The program trained him to act as an investment money manager. Most trainees took six to nine months to pass the necessary tests to be certified to do so, but not Henry. Within three months, Henry had passed all his exams and was managing small stock portfolios for some of the firm's clients. By this time, Kate had given up on her career and was pregnant with their first child. On January 16, 1988, Kate gave birth to an eight-pound baby boy, Henry Larson, Junior. Until that time, Henry and Kate had been living in a small two-bedroom apartment in lower Manhattan. This was

king adults, but both of them felt this was no place to
mes they talked of moving to the suburbs once they
in that environment and were comfortable there.
or home from the hospital, they began searching
home. Henry's parents tried to convince them
r to little Henry's grandparents, but Henry
He was always a loner and didn't want to be
uld pop in whenever they wanted. This was
Kate was in favor of moving closer to Rich-
nsistence won out. This brought Kate and
they and Henry Jr. moved when he was

class" section of New Jersey, and one that
was more than Henry could afford, but his
d both he and Kate decided they would rather
uprooting every time Henry got a better job. So
wi. hard Larson, Henry's father, they purchased a four
bedroom, e-foot home, overlooking the water, paying nearly
$400,000. At first Kate and Henry were hesitant to accept his father's generous
gift, but eventually Henry figured, "What the heck?" Besides, since they bor-
rowed the money from Henry's parents there was no pressure to pay it back right
away. By the summer of '88 Henry, Kate and Henry Junior had packed up and
were on their way from the crowded streets of Manhattan to the quiet suburbs of
South Jersey.

Henry spent three years at Bevel Bressler before he got that same old feeling
again. He got this feeling every time he felt unchallenged by his job and at the
end of his road. He felt he had gone as far as he could there and wanted more. It
simply wasn't enough! This time, however, it was different. In the past, when
Henry got bored he would simply quit. Now he had obligations: a house and a
family to take care of. He just couldn't "up and leave" like he had before. This
time he had to grin and bear it until something better came along. He grudgingly
stayed at Bevel Bressler until the winter of 1989; that's when opportunity presented itself—an opportunity that comes along once in a lifetime and one Henry
wasn't about to let pass him by.

Many thoughts played in young Henry Larson's mind on the morning of February the 3$^{rd}$ in 1989. It was bitter cold that morning, barely 20 degrees, and with
the wind swirling it felt well below zero. But that day a young, brash junior trader
was making his way up to the 99$^{th}$ floor of the World Trade Center for the first

day of his new career. Just days before, Henry's dad, Richard, had introduced him to an old friend from college: Ben Catalano. Catalano was the founder and president of one of the most successful commodity firms in the country: Catalano and Feinberg. By this time there was no longer a "Feinberg" in the company. Sol Feinberg, along with Ben Catalano, started the firm back in 1974, but Catalano bought out his ailing partner in 1983, just one year before Sol—who was a typical two-pack-a-day Wall Street smoker—died of lung cancer. Even after buying Sol out, Ben kept the name as a tribute to his friend and former partner, although by now most people simply referred to the firm as "Catalano." Together, Ben and Sol had slowly built one of the biggest commodity firms in the country. They met while working together as junior brokers themselves. Sol's family had money and funded their original venture, which was an immediate success. In its initial year, the firm's gross was just over two million dollars, with only eleven employees. Now, 15 years later, it had over 200 employees, boasting revenues of over 80 million dollars. The firm was growing at a pace well above even Catalano's expectations. The company sat perched high above the Manhattan skyline on the 99$^{th}$ floor of One World Trade Center in the North Tower.

Ironically, in the past Henry had always declined when it came to meeting any of his father's friends. Henry never saw the need. But in this case, he made an exception. Being a part of Wall Street for three years, Henry now realized who his dad's old friend was. Whereas his father had invited Henry several times in the past, this time Henry wasn't going to let the opportunity pass him by. That evening, Henry tried desperately to impress Catalano. He wanted out of his current job at Bevel Bressler and would do, or say, whatever was necessary to get Ben Catalano to offer him a job. When Henry wanted something, he would stop at nothing to get it. He spent hours trying to impress Catalano. He started by lying, telling Catalano how much he liked his current job, not wanting Catalano to know just how desperate he was. What he didn't realize was that Catalano would have hired him simply because of his relationship with Richard Larson, Henry's father. Still, Henry poured it on, and eventually Catalano took a liking to Henry's aggressiveness. That, and due to his long relationship with his dad, Ben convinced Henry to give up the nine-to-five grind of cold calling and micro-money managing. "I need young, smart, aggressive men I can trust." These words that Catalano spoke would prove to be true, to a fault, in the upcoming years. But Henry seized the opportunity and saw it as a chance to jump at a position with great possible gains, and quick ones at that. One night of ass kissing had gotten him out of his Godforsaken job at Bevel Bressler, and he even got a raise in the process. He would have been happy to take a cut in pay just to be out of Bressler, but getting more money was icing on the cake for Henry. Besides, Ben Catalano was not a young man. At 63, how many more years would he want his "grind" of a job, Henry thought? Henry agreed to take the job, and on that fateful Monday was now exiting the elevator that would bring him, and thousands of others, on a course with destiny.

# CHAPTER 1

▼

# HENRY'S BAPTISM

It didn't take Henry long to learn how to manipulate Ben Catalano. Almost daily he would visit Ben to talk to him about his dad. Catalano rarely took time for such conversations during his busy day in the past, but he seemed eager to chat and relive his boyhood days. Now he had someone to relate those stories to, or so he thought.

"Henry, I hope you had as much fun as me and your dad did in college. I mean, the things we did…" Ben would go on and on and on. Whether it was an all night party or stealing an exam, Ben told Henry all of it. Although Henry had little or no interest, no matter how juicy the story, he was a good listener. He knew this would get him closer to Ben, and that's where he wanted to be. This even more so, when Henry's parents and older sister Susan were tragically killed in a car accident on the Long Island expressway only three months after Henry had joined Ben's firm. Seems one Friday night on the way home from an innocent dinner; a van hopped the divider on the Long Island Expressway, hitting Richard Larson's BMW head on. His car spun and was hit from behind. The metallic mint green convertible flipped over, killing Richard and Beth instantly. As paramedics arrived at the scene, there was little they could do. Richard suffered major trauma, as his head hit the windshield when his car flipped. Most of what was left of his forehead had to be peeled from the glass. Beth, despite having worn her seat belt, was thrown from the car, and by the time she was attended to had lost too much blood to save her. Both were pronounced dead at the scene.

Susan, who was in the back seat, was clinging to life. She also sustained massive trauma and was experiencing internal bleeding. She was rushed to North Shore Hospital with numerous broken bones in her legs. She endured six different surgeries over the next two days, while Henry held vigil for her, but she never even regained consciousness. Henry was by her side when she died, holding her hand until the doctors removed him. He was distraught and angry. This left Henry to care for his younger brother, as he was his last remaining relative. At the time of his parents' and sister's tragic deaths, Glen was away at school in Delaware and had been living there with a friend. By the time Glen got word and traveled back to Long Island, Henry had already dealt with planning his mother and father's funerals. Henry wouldn't let Glen see his sister, as the damage to her face was severe and Henry wanted to insulate his little brother from the sight of her. He told Glen to give it a few days and she would look better, but that never happened. As the youngest, Glen was more upset than Henry. He spent several days at Henry and Kate's house while they tried to come to grips with their loss. Glen wanted to stay and quit school. He was drained, and was leaning on Kate and Henry for support. Kate, being the nurturing person she was, quickly became the big sister Glen had just lost, but Henry wouldn't let his now only remaining family member quit. After a few days, Henry convinced Glen to return to school. He assured Glen that he and Kate were his family now and whatever he needed they would provide for him. As for Henry, he was never that close to his father, but he took his sister's and mother's deaths very hard. Kate, having lost her parents at a young age, tried to comfort Henry, but found him cold and distant. This was the first time Henry had "shut" her out. It was almost as if his heart was hardened by his loss. It was as if this was business for him. He didn't know how to separate the two. He wrapped himself up in his work to help him forget, and this brought Henry even closer to Ben. Ben felt obligated to his now-deceased old buddy, Richard. In a way, Ben and his wife Mary adopted Henry, his family, and Glen as their own. Ben Catalano was that kind of guy. Holidays were now spent with the Catalanos and Ben wouldn't have it any other way. He became "Uncle Ben" to Henry, Jr. This was special for the Catalanos as well. Mary had no brothers or sisters and Ben's only brother was a contractor who built condominiums in Florida. This filled a void in Ben and Mary's lives and they quickly became the family they never had. Kate and Henry now visited them on weekends.

At work, Henry and Ben were spending as much as an hour a day just talking. It didn't take long for Henry to grow weary of Ben's "old boring" stories, but he knew this was a way to keep Catalano's trust and attention. While Ben was rambling about old pranks he and Henry's father pulled and how he started his now prominent company, Henry would pretend to listen, all the while waiting for his turn to "slip in" ideas he had for the firm. And, of course, Ben listened. After all, Henry was the son of Richard Larson who had been one of Ben's oldest and trusted friends. This was one of the reasons Ben had hired him in the first place.

After only six months, Henry started moving up the ladder from junior associate to manager of the firm's options desk. This put Henry on the same level with the other desk managers. These managers noticed that Henry was quickly gaining strength within the firm, and they were jealous of him and his relationship with Ben. But by now he had drained all he could from his chats with "the old man." He needed a new way to impress his boss and achieve the goal he had set for himself. Through their conversations he knew Ben only had a few years left, and that was Henry's timetable to make himself heir to the Catalano throne. This was an extremely high goal to set, but it was the challenge Henry had been searching for his whole life.

In Henry's first year the firm's profits had risen over 25 percent and his desk had become one of the top five producing areas in the company. He became brash and outspoken at meetings. In one particular meeting, Henry attacked the head of futures trading, the firm's most profitable area. The desk was run by Gary Short, who had paid his dues for many years before attaining the status not only as desk manager but senior desk manager. This meant that in Ben's absence, Gary was essentially in charge of running the firm. Gary, too, had his sights set on Ben Catalano's job and saw Henry as a big obstacle. Of course Henry knew all this, which is why he felt the need to challenge Gary in the first place. Besides, being senior desk manager Gary Short was a hulk of a man standing six foot, four inches tall and weighing in at over two hundred and fifty pounds. He resembled a football player more than a Wall Street broker. Henry, on the other hand, was a meek five feet, six inches and barely tipped the scales at one hundred and sixty pounds. Still, Henry was unfazed and continued to attack Gary and his desk. At one point he insinuated Gary's desk was "slipping" and losing business to competing firms.

At that point Gary had heard enough. He took exception to Henry's advances and lunged at him across the conference table. "Who the hell do you think you are? I've been here 15 years and I'm warning you…Fuck with me and I'll bury your little Jewish ass!"

Henry remained cool and laughed, "I'm not Jewish, Gary; I'm Irish."

This only infuriated Gary more. "I swear I'll fuck you up, asshole."

Henry stepped back as the other desk managers tried to restrain Gary. They glared at Henry, and Henry knew they were all on Short's side. If it wasn't for the fact that Ben was watching, Henry figured they all would have let Gary have his wish—that being kicking Henry's ass. They only held him back because they knew Catalano wouldn't approve of such behavior, but now Henry had to think quickly.

He had to find a way to diffuse the situation in his favor.

"Maybe you're right, Gary. Sometimes I guess I get a little carried away, but that's because I feel left out by all of you," he said, pointing at all the desk managers present. "I know what goes on after work and I know I'm not welcome there."

Larson was referring to his being left out of all the gatherings of managers after hours. After most days, the managers would all meet at the Tall Ships, a bar inside the lobby of Two World Trade Center. It was there where they could unwind and get whatever they needed "off their chests." Larson was never invited, as he was seen as "kiss-ass" and all of the other desk heads flat out hated him. But now Short found himself in a quandary. Does he continue fighting with this "asshole" or invite him out and see if they could mend their differences? Besides, as the Senior Desk Manager, wasn't it his responsibility to do this? He, too, knew the top position in the firm would soon be available, and if he could not control such situations, how could Catalano ever see fit to appoint him to run the firm? With Catalano eagerly watching, Gary reluctantly offered his hand to Henry.

"Fine, Henry, you wanna be one of the boys? We'll be at Tall Ships at 5:30, at the back table. Act like an asshole there and there won't be a table of bodies between us."

Henry got Gary's message, loud and clear.

"Great, I'll be there." This was a total victory for Henry. He had tried for months to weasel his way into these little gatherings, with no success. It took a confrontation in front of the boss to finally succeed. Henry quickly headed away from Short and out of the conference room. As he left, Gary Short could only look and wonder if this was the right move. It wouldn't be long before he'd get his answer.

Henry arrived at the Tall Ships at 5:30 on the button that night. He was very quiet and humble, while obviously trying to gain the group's acceptance. Gary was waiting—almost hoping—he would slip-up and say something off-color, anything that could justify Short taking a swing at him, but his chance never came. Henry was the consummate gentleman. No one knew what to think. He even bought several "rounds" of drinks that night. The company bulldog seemed to have neither a bark nor a bite outside the company of his protector: Ben Catalano.

That day, and for the next several weeks, Henry and the other managers consorted in the usual spot in the Tall Ships. They drank beer and vodka, exchanged daily problems and told jokes. Henry was fitting in nicely—too nicely, it seemed. What was once just the guys having drinks and winding down became somewhat of a "bitch" session. It was Henry who suggested it would be better if the managers got their concerns out at these outings.

"Couldn't we help the firm by discussing its problems and trying to find solutions?"

This all made sense to the other managers who were slowly letting Henry into their little "circle of trust." Almost immediately the other managers began bitching about how "Old-Man-Catalano" was living in the past and how he didn't know how to take Catalano Securities to the next level.

One by one they said their pieces and aired out their complaints. Some felt they should be given stock in the firm, while others just felt Ben's ideas on running the firm were old and outdated.

"Look, Catalano is a good man. Personally, I love him, but we're losing business and he refuses to make changes. "He's becoming a dinosaur" is how Gary Short put it. When it was Henry's turn, curiously, he had little or nothing to say. He just liked listening. This went on for several weeks, until at one of the company monthly meetings some of the managers got a little surprise—courtesy of Henry. They were shocked when old Ben Catalano came in to the meeting, looking like a hungry lion.

"So, I understand I'm too old to run this fucking company. Is that right, Gary? How did you put it? I believe I'm a 'fucking dinosaur' now! You piece of shit! I gave you your start in this business and this is how you repay me?"

Short was at a loss for words, as were the others, when Ben attacked them one by one. You see, Henry had gotten them all. He gained their trust just long enough for them to let down their guard. And then he fucked them all. He had found a new way to impress Old Ben and it worked like a charm. Since he never aired any complaints, the other managers had nothing on him. They were left with their mouths hanging open as Ben Catalano took aim at each of them. When the meeting ended, it was clear in Ben Catalano's mind that with the exception of Henry Larson, he perceived all the other prominent desk managers as "disloyal, money grubbing scumbags." Henry had taken another step toward his goal and what he felt was his destiny. Meanwhile, the other desk managers were numb. They were all left wondering how years of loyal service had just been destroyed by this brash new employee of just two years, but they would soon see that this was just the beginning. The worst part was that Henry was using them all as stepping-stones to eventually become their boss. Needless to say, Henry knew in the best interest of staying in one piece never to go into the Tall Ships Bar again. By now most of the firm either hated or envied Henry Larson. This was of no concern to him, because he was moving up the ladder. Even he did not realize his goals would be attained so rapidly.

It was now the summer of '91, and Ben Catalano was about to come to grips with his mortality. On the night of July 10th, his wife Mary called Henry at home, informing him that Ben was in the hospital. Just hours before an ambulance had raced to their upper East Side apartment, responding to Mary's call. Ben had fallen off a chair while watching television, his face twisted in pain and speechless as he reached for his wife's help. Mary quickly called 911. Now, while waiting for help, Mary sat by her husband's side, holding his hand and weeping as he cried for help. The emergency medical technicians started an IV and administered local drugs while quickly loading Ben onto a stretcher. Mary rode with him in the ambulance and never let go of his hand. A few times Ben was able to mutter a few words to her, but that was it. As they arrived at the hospital, Mary had to let Ben go. He was rushed into the emergency room and Mary was ushered to a waiting room. All she could do was think about what might happen. She was a strong-willed woman who had met Ben when they were at Columbia University together. They, like Henry and Kate, married right out of college. They struggled while he was a broker, making a mere $150 a week, and she was a legal assistant, making about the same. As their careers took off, they never had time for kids. But after Ben's childhood friend passed, they treated Henry as if he was their own. While Ben was still the driving force behind Catalano Securities, Mary was as devoted to her charity work as he was to his firm. But now Mary was distraught—a wreck. The only person in her life was fighting for his own life at Roosevelt Hospital in intensive care. Still, she mustered up the strength to fulfill her husband's wishes. Ben felt that Henry was the only one he could trust to run the firm in his absence. Even in his weakened state, he made Mary promise to carry out his desire to have Henry take over.

"Henry, Ben has had a stroke." Henry could hear the quiver in her voice.

"Oh, my God, Mary! Is he all right? Where are you?"

"We're at Roosevelt Hospital. He's in intensive care."

Mary could no longer speak. She choked up and Henry could hear her whimpering as she covered the phone.

"Mary, I'm on my way; don't move!"

Mary pulled it together and stopped Henry. "No, Henry, I'm all right. There is nothing you can do here. Stay home; be with your family."

"But what about Ben, Mary? Is he gonna make it?"

"We don't know, but more important is we need you to run the firm for now."

Henry paused, grinning sheepishly. He thought, *thank God she can't see me.* "Are you kidding, Mary? Why me?"

"Henry, a memo is being drawn up and will be distributed shortly to the firm's desk heads. This is how Ben wants it. It's something we talked about several times. He felt you eventually would run the firm when he retired, but now we can't wait. We need you, Henry." Henry paused briefly.

"I won't let you down, Mary. I promise. I'll take good care of everything." These were words that brought comfort to Mary that night, but they would prove to be one of many lies Henry would use to move in on Ben and his firm.

The next morning Henry rushed to Roosevelt Hospital to check on Ben. Mary had stayed all night in the waiting room, slipping in and out of a light sleep. When she saw Henry, she began to cry. Henry held her strongly; assuring her Ben would be all right. The doctors told her they would know more in the morning and she was waiting for their verdict. Henry stayed with Mary for several hours before the answer came. A young, tall doctor made his way toward them just before 11:00 a.m.

"Are you Mrs. Catalano?"

"Yes," Mary responded.

"Your husband has had a massive edema. He's still unconscious and we are running tests to see how much damage was done. Our main concern is that he had several other small strokes during the night."

Mary was confused and Henry took over.

"What are you saying, Doctor? In English, please!"

"I'm sorry; he's had a very large stroke—one that has taken a very big toll on him...He's in bad shape. All we can do is hope."

Henry hugged Mary and took her out of the hospital. He had already called Kate and she was on her way into the city. She would take over for Henry and stay with Mary. Henry convinced Mary to get some coffee and toast as they waited for Kate. Henry, once again, assured her of his commitment to her and Ben. Kate arrived and walked Mary back to the hospital. Henry kissed them both good-bye and headed back downtown. All the way, the doctor's words replayed in his mind. He never said anything to Mary, but he was sure the doctor was telling them to read between the lines. He was sure Ben would not survive this.

Henry moved quickly so as not to lose his opportunity. As his mentor was slowly dying, Henry was positioning himself for his ultimate triumph. In the following days he removed three key board members who opposed his every move and replaced them with loyal subordinates. As it was hard to find three people who actually liked him, he preyed on those who harbored the most resentment for Old Ben. When he was finished—in just two short weeks—he had succeeded in gaining controlling power over the board that, in Ben's absence, had absolute power to make company policy. It was written into the company by-laws that should the CEO become incapacitated, the board had the power to make all decisions until a new CEO was appointed. Having that power, they would, of course, make their first order of business to select a new CEO in Ben's absence. Just in case Old Ben should somehow recover enough to want to resume his position, Henry quickly convened the board of Catalano Securities and had them declare Ben unfit. Once that was done, they named Henry the new CEO. Henry had to make some pretty big promises to a few board members to convince them to do this, but in the end it was well worth it. Henry had achieved what he had set out to do. In just 2 ½ years at Catalano, he attained his ultimate goal. He did all of this while Ben lay helpless in Roosevelt Hospital, near death, completely unaware of what was happening. Henry kept telling Mary Catalano "all was good." By the time Ben passed away, on August 4th, Mary Catalano, completely unaware of Henry's betrayal to both her and Ben, had lost both her husband and his firm. This hurt almost as much as losing Ben. Not only had she lost her husband, but her family as well, betrayed by a boy she treated as a son, someone she put all her faith and trust in a time of need. Henry trampled all over it. Needless to say, there were very little words ever spoken between Henry and Mary again.

Mary and her lawyers fought Henry in an attempt to regain power of the firm, but with the board behind Henry, she had no chance. In the end she accepted the board's offer of a buyout. When Ben died, all Mary wanted was to keep the dream of his firm alive, but Henry made sure that wouldn't happen. Mary Catalano, with no other alternative, buried herself in the long list of charities she had long been involved with. She never visited the Trade Center or Catalano and Feinberg again.

Henry was elated. In just two years he had gone from junior associate to running what was now the second largest commodities firm in the country. The fact that he did it at the expense of his father's best friend and his mentor was of no issue to him. Just to add insult to injury, Henry didn't attend Ben Catalano's funeral. Fearing Mary wouldn't allow him anyway, he took the position of refusing to go. He didn't want the firm's employees to confirm what was already extremely obvious by being turned away at the funeral. So, he insisted on staying away, claiming he was "too busy," but he did send flowers. They were daisies, I believe.

# CHAPTER 2

▼

# WELCOME THE NEW KING

As Henry Larson was reveling in his new appointment as CEO of Catalano Securities, much to his surprise his employees were plotting a mass exodus. When word of this leaked to some of the board members, they quickly convened in Henry's office. Rick Stein, who was one of Henry's new loyal appointees, quickly assessed the situation to Henry.

"Henry, if these people leave we're fucked. It will only be the beginning. Shit! How will it look to the rest of those who stay? I mean you just took over. It's a fucking disaster! We have to find a way to make them believe you can run this firm."

"Believe in me?"

"Believe in me!" Henry shot back.

"That's right, Henry. No one out there believes in you. Like it or not, you haven't made many friends or allies since you've been here."

"What would you have me do, Rick? Kiss their asses, maybe?"

"It's not the worst idea you've ever had, Henry. Besides, we need these people. They represent our revenues."

"Fuck those guys, Rick," Henry mumbled, "Shit, they're nothing more than order takers. They sit there like Pavlov's dogs, waiting for their customers to ring their dinner bells. I've been out there. Remember? They're a dime a dozen. We could toss them out tomorrow and get one hundred other idiots off the street to do the same job. Who the fuck do they think they are?" Henry was livid and continued mumbling obscenities before finishing his tirade. "Besides, who do they think they are fooling with? If they try leaving here, we can tie them up in court for years. They'll be living under bridges before I'm done with them. Tell them that, Rick. See what they say once they know what I'm capable of."

Rick just shook his head. "And you wonder why they don't wanna work for you, huh, Henry?"

Henry paused while trying to regain his composure. This was all new to him. On the outside he was trying to appear tough while staying composed, but inside he was pissed. Truly, on the inside he was scared! He had worked so hard, screwed so many people to get to where he was, and his first order of business was to try not to lose the whole damn company in under a week. He never contemplated people leaving the firm. He needed time to figure it out.

"You calm them down, Rick. You keep them around for a few more days and I'll figure this thing out. After all, it can't be too tough. They're just a bunch of drunken morons." With that, Henry angrily whisked all of the board members out of his office and began his plotting. He only had a few days. That's all his board could buy him with this many disgruntled employees.

Over the next few days, Henry barely left his office. He was entrenched in his quest to not lose his business. He refused to speak to even desk managers for their opinions, as he felt they, too, were below his level of thinking. But true to his word, on the third day Henry was ready to detail to all desk heads and board members the outline of a plan—one that would keep the brokers from leaving Catalano.

Henry had convened a meeting of all desk managers in the boardroom of the firm. By now most of them were convinced of their imminent departure. Before Henry arrived, most of them separated into little "cliques," discussing what firms they would go to once this meeting ended. Henry strolled into the room and sat at the head of the table. He looked down, but very few faces were looking back at him. Most were looking at each other or down at the floor, as they couldn't look him in the face. Henry peered up and down both sides of the twenty-foot mahogany conference table, taking time to look at every single desk manager. He had no fear and was assessing who in the room was strong-willed enough to look back at him. Now it was time, and as the murmurs quieted, Henry spoke.

"As of this day, the top fifty producers in Catalano Securities will be offered a chance to become partners in the firm." You could have heard a pin drop. Henry paused again, peering up and down at every desk manager. This time they were all looking back. Could it be that the hated Henry Larson was going to offer employees what the late Ben Catalano had always refused?

He continued. "That's right, I'm offering a piece of the action to all of you." He then proceeded to trash the only thing left of the late Ben Catalano: his reputation. "Catalano was a great man, but when it came to this—the growth of his business—he was a dinosaur. Gary had it right." He was referring to Gary Short's assessment of Ben back in the days of the Tall Ships meetings. "He never understood your needs. As producers, you were entitled to this, and he shut you out. I know many of you think I'm the bad guy, but maybe now you can see the big picture behind my actions; that is to preserve this company and you, its foundation."

This was an odd turn of events from a guy who just 72 hours earlier referred to his "foundation" of brokers as "a dime a dozen order takers" and "drunken morons"! Nevertheless, none of the brokers knew he said those words, and therefore did not know how Henry truly felt about them. As for the plan, it was a huge hit. However, Henry still had to sell the terms of the partnership to the "would-be suckers," as he secretly called them. Once the managers and top producers were sold on Henry's offer to keep them on board, he slowly spoon-fed them the terms of their partnership. Each would have to put up $200,000 for their shares. For most top guys, this was not a problem, but for about 15—or one third—of them, it was too expensive. They simply did not have that kind of available cash. That was no problem for their new loveable boss. He simply offered them a one-year/interest-free loan. If they could not pay the loan back in that time period, he would offer a new loan at a mere 5% interest yearly. Henry simply would have the payments taken out of their salaries on a monthly basis. It would be that simple. He assured his new partners that within three, maybe four years, they would not only recover their initial investment, but would reap a healthy profit. As most of them saw how the firm's numbers were soaring, this all made sense, and thus it was an easy sell. Amazingly, none of them even asked to see the company books, not that Henry would have shown them. Still, one would have thought with what was at stake someone would have at least asked.

Most of them didn't bother to read, or just ignored the fine print on these partnerships. Few noticed the clause telling them if they left for a competing firm in the future they would lose their $200,000, or that their note or loan was callable-on-demand if they fell into disfavor with the firm. This meant that the firm, at any time, could demand payment in full. The employee would have but ten days to come up with the money. Henry knew that if they could do that, they wouldn't need him to give them a loan in the first place. This gave him tremendous leverage with these employees. Henry was sure that once he got them to trust him, even for just a minute, he would find a way to swing the deal in his favor. He surely accomplished that. Offering them partnerships was something very few could resist, no matter what the terms. As for Henry, he was delighted with himself. After all, he had just raised ten million dollars in additional capital on partnerships that would prove in the future to be of little value, and by doing so he kept all his key employees. He was very proud of himself. Henry had just learned how vulnerable even his best employees were, and he would use this to his advantage for as long as they worked for him.

As the fiscal year of 1991 ended, accountants were bringing the bad news to all of Catalano Securities new partners. Not only did the partnership fail to make money, somehow it operated at a loss, despite doing a staggering 210 million dollars in gross revenues. This was done with some very creative accounting. The company was actually seeking more money from the partners in the form of a "capital call," but that wasn't the worst news. Only now were most partners learning that they were hostages in their own firm. If they tried to leave, not only would they forfeit their $200,000 partnership money, they could be sued so as not to compete with Catalano for a period of no less than one year. If they stayed, they were at the mercy of whatever compensation Henry Larson deemed fair. It was all in the contract. They simply acted as Henry had predicted. They wanted to be partners of the firm so badly that they would have signed any agreement— even one that screwed them—like this one. Few had the stomach or financial wherewithal to escape. And well, with his employees nestled comfortably under his thumb, now Henry could be himself. No more "Mr. Nice Guy." He could be his usual self: a real prick. The brokers did score a small victory when they revolted against putting up more money for their partnerships. Henry had the books amended so as not to follow through on his request for the partners to pony up more money. It was a small concession for such a great victory, Henry figured. No new money would have to be paid into the partnerships, but no dividends would be paid out, either. This would be the case year after year after year after year. The only casualty of Henry's creative accounting was the company's CPA, Mike Santoli. He resigned rather than go along with Henry's illegal doctoring of the books. So Henry simply hired one that would.

Going forward, Henry's most challenging dilemma was to make sure there were no profits reported by Catalano Securities each year. That was usually taken care of with huge payouts to select personnel, including a hefty 30-million-dollar bonus paid to himself in the first year. But Catalano's revenues were still soaring and Henry needed another outlet. Despite the hard work his employees did creating these profits, Henry felt they were all overpaid. He simply refused to share the firm's profits with people he had little or no respect for. He constantly used the money to venture into new businesses. If it failed, he didn't care, as it wasn't his money they were risking anyway. The problem was most of the ventures were succeeding and Catalano's profits were getting harder to hide, so Henry decided it was time to take the firm to a new level. It was time for Catalano Securities to go global. To do this, Henry hired Len Abraham. Abraham would be in charge of all overseas operations. Abraham had previously held a similar position for RJM, Inc., a London-based bond-trading house. Abraham, a graduate of Wharton Business School, had over twenty years experience on Wall Street. Henry had had some "run-ins" with Len in the past, but always respected his ability to run an operation. Besides, Len knew a lot of the traders and brokers, both in the United States and abroad. This would be invaluable in the hiring process. Since Abraham was divorced, with no children, he lived for his job. This was another quality that drew Henry to him. Henry loved having someone who would be happy to devote twenty-four hours a day to his work. As a well-connected and respected executive for twenty years, Henry had a man who also knew all the people who could help cut through the red tape of doing business abroad. Abraham didn't come cheap, but Henry still had all that partnership money to spend and profits to hide.

It didn't take long for Abraham to become a success. Just as Henry had thought, Len was able to put together a team of experienced well-respected brokers. With Henry's blessing, Len spared no expense in doing so. Henry had "opened the vault" for Len to overpay brokers from other firms in order to lure them into working for Catalano. It was the way business was done on Wall Street, and the fastest way to "steal" business from competitors was to steal their best brokers. It was a mere matter of months and Catalano Securities' business was quickly rising worldwide. Whether it was London, Tokyo or Malaysia, they stormed into the commodities and futures industry like no other American firm before them. The only problem with Catalano Securities' quick success was that this presented Henry with yet another problem: how could he possibly hide all those new profits? That required yet another new venture, and Henry made it a priority to find one. Henry met with the board in the fall of 1992 to unveil the firm's newest, most exciting venture ever. It was at that meeting that Henry announced, "Catalano is going to become automated."

He explained that the future is an automated, error-free system where traders can execute all trades on their own—electronically, with the touch of a button. It would be that quick and without the possibility of human error. Most members of the board, including the loyalists like Rick Stein, were quick to point out the potential backlash of the brokers once it got out that this system would make them obsolete! Henry, as usual, was prepared to address the problem.

"First of all, Rick, this project will take years and millions of dollars. Second, there is no reason for them to know about it until we are ready to launch the program to our customers, and when that time comes, the brokers will do as they're told. It is up to all of you to assure them that this will not affect their positions in the firm, and ultimately, as partners, they will reap the rewards with us."

"What about the ones that aren't that fucking gullible?" snapped Gary Short.

"Well, we'll just have to remind them of the agreements they signed. Make sure they fully understand how hard I will fuck them if they don't go along with the program."

Gary looked up at Henry, "So, its fuck me now or fuck me later."

Henry ignored him and left the board members to themselves, thinking what a perfect scenario this was for him. He now had all the brokers under his thumb, where he could squash them at any time. This excited Henry more than making money. He reveled in his power over people. And now he was building the ultimate broker "dooms-day" machine. Meanwhile, as the fiscal year came to a close Catalano Securities recorded its largest production numbers ever, grossing over 300 million dollars. Besides the news of their impending doom, the lame duck brokers could do nothing but shake their heads when the company once again somehow recorded no profits for that year. This, of course, was because Henry had cleverly put would-be profits into an account for the building of his prize electronic trading system. As the year 1993 approached, Henry had a gift for the firm: his brother Glen. Glen Larson was five years younger than Henry, and after graduating from Delaware had spent the better part of his life jumping from job to job. Unlike his older brother, he liked late nights and had several girlfriends. Glen would be in charge of overseeing the development of the new electronic system Henry was developing.

When told of the news, Gary Short sarcastically told Rick Stein, "Great, this will give people someone else to hate on the days Henry is out."

# CHAPTER 3

▼

# THE ATTACK OF '93

On the morning of February 26th, there was a chill in the air. Temperatures barely reached 30 degrees that day, but things were about to heat up in the World Trade Center. Shortly after 9:00 am, a van carrying several hundred pounds of explosives entered its parking garage. The van traveled down several floors of the garage before parking. Its cowardly occupants, having parked the van hastily, exited the area. A few minutes later the towers rocked and swayed as an explosion filled both buildings with thick black smoke. Outside on West Street, as smoke poured out of the buildings, there was chaos everywhere, while inside, the building's elevators automatically shut down. To their credit, there was very little panic among the people within the towers. Most people weren't even sure what was happening. This, in itself, probably saved lives. After realizing that there had, in fact, been an explosion, some forty to fifty thousand people slowly walked down one flight of stairs after another to the safety of several hundred waiting police and fire workers. The employees of Catalano Securities were among those who endured the longest journey—some three-and-a-half hours long. They did so by forming groups of ten and twelve and by putting wet paper towels over their faces to shield them from the smoke and heat. Several groups were formed as they uniformly made their way down almost 100 floors. Even the stairwells were completely black with smoke and most of the emergency lights were not functioning. This made their trip down all the more difficult, as well as frightening. So as not to fall all over each other, people counted the steps as they walked down. There were eleven steps between each floor. Slowly, for several hours, that was the only sound that could be heard. "One—two—three—four—five—six—seven—eight—nine—ten—eleven—turn." The sound went on for hours. At one point a few stopped, insisting that they couldn't go on. There were a few of the heavier-set men who by the 40th or so floor found it almost impossible to breathe, but they all stopped giving enough pause to reinforce their co-workers and force them to push on. "We're in this together" yelled out Eddie Macanee, a former football player at Rutgers. "We're going down as a group, so everyone, let's move." Then once again the counting began, "one—two—three..." etc. It was done incredibly orderly and with great calm, especially under the circumstances. Eddie was one of the more outspoken partners at Catalano. He had no fear of Henry, because he was not afraid of any wrath Henry could bring upon him. He was one of the few who were financially secure, wisely being frugal with his money rather than spending it like a drunken sailor as most others were guilty of. So he was a leader for them—one they could stand behind. He reinforced them every few flights down. This helped occupy people's minds as well. There was no panic as they finished counting their 1,078 steps to the waiting fresh air. By the time they actually reached the outside of the building, the thirty-degree temperature was a welcome breeze. They sucked up the fresh air, thanking each other—and God—that they had survived. Most could barely stand once they reached the lobby. During their journey down, many feared they would not survive. Thoughts of their loved ones and prayers danced in their heads, but now they were on the ground floor, just a few feet from the safety of waiting EMS workers. By the grace of God, every one of them had escaped with little or no injury, not physically at least.

Some arrived with clothes completely black, including their undergarments. It was truly a miracle, they thought. This incident in itself defined the closeness that these people had developed over the years with each other. They were unified. For the past three years their fate had been in the hands of a man who despised their mere existence. Until that day they had never realized how that made them stronger and brought them closer. As fate would have it, Henry wasn't around that day. He chose that week to visit Len Abraham in their London office. Still, the attack on February 26th posed some problems for Henry. Several key employees balked at returning to the towers for fear of future attacks—a fear even Henry was experiencing. Even though he escaped the ordeal of February 26th, Henry was hesitant to simply walk back in there.

The attack, as it turned out, had been orchestrated by a group of Arab terrorists known as the "Al Qaida." Their leader was Osama Bin Laden, the son of a wealthy Saudi Arabian. Ironically, the United States and Bin Laden were allies against the Russians several years earlier, but since then his own father had cast Bin Laden out of Saudi Arabia. He became obsessed with the United States. He did not like their presence in the Arab nation and quickly became the new leader of this terrorist group aimed at teaching Americans, as he put it, to "stay away and mind their own business." He felt America was only interested in defending Israel. As one who despised Jews, this only strengthened his hatred towards the United States. This attack was his first attempt at demonstrating his willingness to show Americans that he meant business, by attacking innocent men, women and children with indifference as to whom or how many he could kill. Seven members of his group were eventually convicted of this crime and sent to prison for life. Bin Laden, however, was never brought to justice. He would continue his quest to inflict as much fear, pain and death as possible to Americans around the world.

# CHAPTER 4

▼

# STARTING OVER

In the coming months, while working in temporary quarters away from the World Trade Center which was under extensive repair, Henry became very "politically popular," attending charities and making donations to local politicians campaigns. Henry had always had an interest in politics. Now, as head of a large prestigious Wall Street firm, he was well received by political fund seekers. Henry donated funds on behalf of Catalano in order to gain access to many local politicians. This led him to meet Jim Swimhammer.

Jim Swimhammer had graduated in the top of his class at Pennsylvania University. He was a good-looking single man who looked more like a professional athlete than an attorney. Still young and somewhat inexperienced, at age 28 he had a hunger for the "big time."

While attending a political fundraiser, Henry was introduced to the handsome six-foot, two-inch tall, brown-haired, brown-eyed attorney. Swimhammer had served two years as legal counsel for a small time local assemblyman. In their brief conversation, Henry clearly observed how unhappy Jim was in his current position. Henry clear in making it knew him that his current position left him without a challenge. This was something Henry could relate to. Swimhammer went out of his way to impress Henry with his legal background and tried to convince him what an asset he could be to a firm such as Catalano and Feinberg. What intrigued Henry the most, though, was Jim's last name.

"Swimhammer. That's not a common name now. Would you somehow be related to Ken Swimhammer?" asked Henry.

"You bet," Jim said with a smile, sensing he finally had Henry's attention.

Ken Swimhammer was head of all overseas central intelligence for the United States, answering only to the president. He had served in that position for over twelve years, lasting through two presidencies. He was well respected as a military genius, with more information at his disposal that anyone in the United States military. He was, without a doubt, quietly one of the most powerful men in America, and here was Henry, chatting with his little brother.

They exchanged a few more pleasantries while Henry desperately tried to pry information from him. After about ten minutes, Jim realized Henry's only interest was in his brother Ken, and excused him.

"Nice meeting you, Mr. Larson."

Henry asked for and received Jim's business card. "I may need someone like you, Jim."

Jim paused while trying to measure Henry up. He wasn't sure if Henry was serious, or just bullshitting him. Still, he cordially answered Henry. "Well, you know where to find me." And with that Jim handed Henry his card, but dismissed Henry's interest as a professional courtesy. He would soon find out he was wrong. It would be less than a week before Henry would meet Jim Swimhammer again; this time under much different circumstances.

First, Henry had to deal with getting his employees either back into the World Trade Center or find new office space. Henry had brought in some top legal minds to have at his disposal. After sifting through days of Catalano's lease documents, they reported that they felt Catalano Securities could escape their lease, due to a questionably worded disaster clause. Henry immediately started searching for a new location. The Port Authority, Catalano's landlord and owner of the Trade Center, threatened to sue Henry and Catalano if they left, but Henry's high-priced lawyers assured him that they would have little trouble defeating the Port Authority in court. So, Henry decided, "we're moving." After meeting with board members, it was clear that many employees did not want to return to the building they felt defenseless in. While Henry quietly all but locked up space uptown on the 29th and 30th floors of the new Met Life building that was once the old Pan AM Building, opportunity once again knocked on Henry Larson's door. The Port Authority, now desperate, made a last ditch effort to keep its largest and longest tenant. It seemed they feared that if Catalano Securities exercised its "escape" clause, it would open up the floodgates for several other firms to do the same. Besides, whom would they get to fill that space after what had just happened? On the flip side, if the Port Authority could keep Catalano as a tenant, it might put other tenants at ease. They offered Catalano a 30% rent reduction for 10 years! While Henry was certainly intrigued by the offer, he was no fool. He smelled blood and went in for the kill. He told them it was a 50% discount for 20 years or Catalano Securities would never return to the towers. Suddenly, the fears of his employees and even himself fell by the wayside. I mean, not only were we talking about saving over 20 million dollars, but also Henry truly enjoyed watching top executives of the "mighty" Port Authority squirm at his feet. With no other options, the Port Authority agreed to Henry's terms. The only problem was how would he tell his employees they would have to return to the building that just a month ago almost did them in—the building that, as far as terrorists were concerned, had a big 'bulls-eye' on it. There were already several employees in therapy. It's not as if he could say he knew how they felt. He didn't have to trek down 99 floors in thick black smoke for almost four hours! While there were suffering that fate, he was enjoying a quiet lunch with Len Abraham in London. He would have to at least act sincere in his quest to get them back into the building. He figured if things went bad, if the employees threatened not to return, he would simply pull out his trump card: that good old partnership agreement. He relied on his gut feeling that not enough of his employees would have "the balls" to challenge him by quitting, and he was right.

When it was time, he masterfully and somberly addressed his firm. "We put some of the greatest legal minds to work on this problem. Personally, I want no part of going back there either, but there is nothing we can do. Our lease is iron-clad." Only his brother, Glen, knew of the deal Henry had made with the Port Authority. As he listened to Henry speak, even he marveled at his brother's performance, after which he praised him. "Bro, I learned something today."

"What's that?" Henry asked.

"You're kidding, right? I mean how the hell do you fuck people so hard with that 'puppy-dog-I'm-so-sorry' look. People actually believed you out there."

"Glen, my little brother, it's very easy when you're dealing with people like them. Its not like they had a choice." The Larson boys both chuckled. As Glen left Henry's office, he tried to regain his composure so as not to be seen laughing by the other employees.

Still, Henry did have some reservations about returning to the World Trade Center. His next official move was to call on Jim Swimhammer, the man he met just five days ago. Swimhammer, being the brother of the man with more information than any other man in the United States except the president himself, was a man Henry wanted working for him. With Jim on the payroll, if there was any future terrorist threats Henry might have some protection having him around. Besides, either way Jim would have lots of information the rest of the world would not. And, if he had it, that meant Henry would have it as well. Needless to say, this more than excited a man who thrived on power like Henry did.

Henry met Swimhammer at Catalano's temporary office on the morning of April 1st. Although he downplayed his interest in hiring him, he let Swimhammer ramble on about what value he could bring to Henry and his company. Funny thing was, Henry wanted to hire him before he even sat down, but true to form, he made him squirm a little before offering him the job.

"What exactly would you expect of me?" Swimhammer asked.

"I need a consultant."

"I'm not a consultant; I'm an attorney. Besides, you can get a consultant anywhere. Why me?"

"Because I need one with your connections, that's why." Henry certainly wasn't one to pull any punches, Swimhammer thought to himself.

"Mr. Larson, I can't guarantee my relationships will always give me information." Now it was Swimhammer who was being cute with Henry, but Henry wasn't biting and immediately let him know what he was in for.

"Well, the job pays $200,000 a year for someone with knowledge. However, should you become uh…stupid, let's say, then you're about as valuable to me as a pencil. Would that be a clear enough job description? Do we understand each other?" Henry smiled at Jim.

At that moment, Jim Swimhammer knew two things. As long as his brother held his position as head of overseas central intelligence, he would have a high-paying position in Catalano Securities. But should his brother lose his job, they might as well open a pizzeria somewhere together, because they would both be unemployed. Regardless, Jim took the job, figuring he might as well "take the money." His current position only paid him about $80,000 a year and Catalano was a much bigger firm with more opportunity.

Swimhammer made his first official move to convince Henry to purchase loss-of-business insurance. This was a policy that would protect the firm in case of any type of business interruption. For example, Catalano would have been reimbursed for every penny it lost while it was "shut down" due to the Trade Center bombing. For days Jim and Henry argued over the cost of such a policy. It was tough for Jim. Henry wouldn't give ice to an Eskimo in a snowstorm, so paying an insurance premium of $250,000 a year seemed ridiculous, especially after they had already escaped the potential disaster. Besides, Henry had now built a temporary office site, and he intended to keep it for any such potential future problems. So why would he need this insurance, especially at that price? In the end, Jim was able to convince him how valuable this policy could be.

"You see, the way it works, Henry, is as follows. If the firm has to close for any reason—fire, flood, power outage, etc.—the company would receive whatever their average day of revenues was for up to 60 days. Even if you keep these temporary offices, if you average less business while here they have to pay you the difference. You can't tell me you haven't lost some revenues since you've been here."

This started to make sense to Henry. Catalano had lost about 15% of its normal revenues over a period of two months. Their temporary setup consisted of slower, antiquated computers and systems. Customers have very little patience during a busy trading day to take the time to wait. Consequently, they go elsewhere. Regardless, such a number amounted to about seven and half million dollars! Now Henry wanted to know more. If this policy did what Jim claimed, he could have collected over seven million dollars without having to pay the brokers a dime of it.

"What else does this insurance do for us?"

"If you can prove any singular act causes you to lose revenues permanently, the policy pays a onetime payment of two times your previous year's revenue."

"You mean if the company is rendered permanently incapacitated I get twice last year's revenues—almost three quarters of a billion dollars)?"

"That's right, and that's why you want this policy, Henry."

Henry smiled. He thought that even though he had just hired Jim, he was already paying immediate dividends to him. Best of all, this was their little secret. Other board members were not privy to this meeting or its outcome. Henry couldn't resist the possibilities, so it came to be that Catalano secured the policy, although never really expecting to capitalize on its value. It was like a lottery ticket to Henry. Once again, he would fund the policy with profits he needed to hide. Even if they never collected a dime, the brokers were "footing the bill." Ironically, if he did ever collect anything, the brokers wouldn't ever even know it or be able to collect on it.

May 10th, 1993 was an unusually warm sunny day in Manhattan. It was not so bright for the many who had to go to work that day for Catalano Securities. This was the day the World Trade Center was to reopen its doors. Many employees dreaded making the trip up to the 99th floor. With the exception of a few who would never return to that building, one by one Catalano employees made their way on to and up the elevators. They were back! Henry was especially happy that day. Although he appeared somber on the outside so as to sympathize with his employees, he was delighted with himself. That was the day his rent was cut in half, more money that no one knew about. I mean, he wasn't supposed to pass that savings on to his brokers, was he? Those who actually did suffer that cold February morning, the ones that spent some three to four hours painfully walking down 99 floors in a congested, smoke-filled stairway, not knowing if they would even survive. No, sir, they didn't deserve to share or even know of such money.

# CHAPTER 5

▼

# TERROR IN THE SKIES

Over the next several years, things were relatively quiet at Catalano Securities. The firm was slowly growing to monster proportions. Len Abraham was a huge success overseas and the development of the electronic trading systems was almost complete. As the business grew, so did participation in the partnership program. There were now over 300 partners in the firm and over 700 employees worldwide. While this was prosperous for Henry, it was not so special for the original 50 partners. Not only did they not receive any dividends on their original investment for years, but also now the value of their shares were being diluted with every new partner. Henry continued to pay himself and other select officers big bonuses, while sinking the rest of the company profits into accelerating his long awaited electronic trading system. The firm had now invested a staggering 100 million into the venture. Of course Henry didn't mind. After all, it wasn't his money. He was still using the partnership profits to finance it. How ironic that his own employees were paying for the very instrument that would one day make their jobs obsolete.

As the summer of '96 approached, the system was only months away from completion. It was time to start planning the transition of brokers to machines. Henry knew he had to tread gently on that ground.

Although he had very little respect for his brokers, he knew not to insult their customers. To be successful in transforming his business to electronic trading required not pissing off the customers and their relationships with their brokers.

He would have to convince them all that this move would be beneficial to all, even his brokers.

While all of this was playing itself out in Henry's mind, one August evening fate was once again about to take center stage. It was on August 8th of 1996, at about 9:30 pm that Henry and his wife Kate sat at home watching the news. Kate moved around, obviously uncomfortable, as she was eight months pregnant with their second child. They were watching Fox News Network's "Hannity and Colmes,'" as they did every night when a disturbing report came across the television screen. A plane had crashed off the east coast of Long Island. At the time, this seemed like a meaningless unrelated matter to Henry, but it would prove to be an incident that opened the door to life-changing events that would follow. As the night went on, with reports of several hundred casualties, Henry actually seemed annoyed at the constant interruptions, as almost all television stations had now "cut" to the story. Tired and bored, Henry called it a night, turning off the television set and going to bed.

Meanwhile, off the coast of eastern Long Island, rescue workers and police were frantic. There were plane fragments and fire everywhere. The burning plane's fuel lit up the water like a runway for almost one full mile. The FBI rushed to the scene as some witnesses reported some kind of light—or a flash—heading toward the plane before it exploded. The fires burned on the water as a grim reminder, until morning. Over the next several days, pieces of the plane, along with casualties, were slowly dragged from the water. There were no survivors. Over 200 people died that night. The man heading up the investigation for the FBI was Jack Konnor. Konnor, in fact, held the highest position within the FBI in all of New York. That night, while investigators brought Konnor up to speed on the situation, they told him of several witnesses who had come forward. Some had stayed around for hours, waiting. The agents who originally interviewed them asked them to wait for Konnor. They wanted their boss to hear their accounts of the accident he, but Konnor seemed to want no part of them. At first he simply refused to consider their accounts.

"What are they going to tell me?" an annoyed Konnor asked. "That a plane exploded? We can all see that!"

Konnor was somewhat surprised at what his agents said next. Apparently at least four of these witnesses, unrelated to each other, made the same claim: that a rocket or a missile appeared to streak across the sky, striking the plane and taking it down in a ball of flames. Konnor listened to their accounts while preparing for his first of many press conferences. He then instructed his field agents to take names and telephone numbers and to send the witnesses home.

"Tell them we'll get back to them."

"Why are we sending material witnesses home?" one of his agents made the mistake of asking.

Konnor proceeded to give him a full two-minute dissertation on who was in charge of the investigation, after which the agent sheepishly left and carried out his orders. Konnor went on the air that night, telling all of America how an intense investigation had already begun.

"We will find out how this aircraft was taken down." Those were curious words, to say the least. "We will provide a most thorough open investigation, with daily reports. I promise we will get answers to what happened and bring to justice anyone who may have had any involvement if wrongdoing is found."

Ironically, Konnor then asked that any witnesses who may have seen something come forward immediately and said that every minute was critical.

"The first 24 hours are critical in an investigation such as this. We need to talk to witnesses while things are still fresh in their minds."

He made these statements just minutes after sending some of these critical witnesses home. Field agents looked at each other inquisitively, wondering what their boss was up to. Over the next several days, there were all kinds of wild rumors as to what happened that night over Long Island. One story had the military conducting training exercises, accidentally shooting down the plane. Another had terrorists using ground-to-air missiles, hitting the jet. Then, of course, there was the story the FBI was slowly feeding the country—the one that ultimately would become official—that a faulty wire created a spark, igniting fuel within the wing of the plane and causing a massive explosion. The FBI explained that no such military training exercises existed that night and any streaking light seen was probably some kind of spark created by the plane just prior to the explosion. These conclusions were arrived upon after putting what was left of the plane back together in a remote airplane hangar off the coast of eastern Long Island. Very few people were allowed into the hangar during the procedure. Once fully put together, the plane was immediately disassembled, fueling speculation of some kind of cover-up. Konnor, on a daily basis, dismissed the other accounts of that evening as people's imaginations running wild. While all of the country was left to wonder if what the FBI was telling them was the real story or not, Henry Larson was about to find out the truth for himself.

The very next day following the crash, or explosion, of TWA Flight 800, while Henry was sitting in his office, in strolled Jim Swimhammer. Jim was about to tell Henry an amazing tale.

"Morning, Henry. What are you reading?"

"Ah, this plane crashed last night. What a terrible tragedy!" Henry said, trying to act as if he cared.

"What crash?" asked Jim

"Jesus, Jim! Are you in a coma or something? It's all over the television and in the papers. It lit up Long Island last night like the fourth of July!!"

"Oh sure, I know about that, but it wasn't no crash."

"Crash, explosion—whatever, Jim."

"No, what I meant was that it was no accident."

As Henry was about to challenge Jim, he sensed that Jim knew something from the smirk on his face. Henry remembered this was the exact reason he had hired Jim. Henry jumped from his office chair, closed his office door and went right at Swimhammer.

"What do you think you know, Jim?"

Jim sipped his coffee, placed his cup on Henry's desk and gave Henry a knowing smile. He then spent the next half hour filling him in on all the details. It was probably the longest Henry had ever gone without interrupting someone's conversation. He was mesmerized, as Jim gave him details only the highest-ranking officials would know. Hell, not even the Governor of New York was getting this much information! It seemed that both rumored stories were somewhat true. The Navy was in the area that night, but they were not on a training mission. They were responding to reports of a possible terrorist attack with a missile or a bomb of some sort. In fact, all planes had been diverted from that airspace for that very reason, although they were told it was a military training exercise. However, this particular plane—Flight 800—made the fatal mistake of coming too close, and from a deserted section of Fire Island the attack took place. In fact, not one but two missiles were fired that night, one striking the wing of the plane igniting its fuel supply and finally causing the massive explosion and death of all on board. The Navy was able to move in and apprehend the attackers, quickly leaving before local law enforcement showed up.

"Bullshit!" was Henry's initial response. "If we caught the bastards, why aren't we parading them in front of the country? Why the secret?"

"We don't know who they represent yet. They think it's that scumbag, Bin Laden, but they're not sure. And here's something else. That plane was on the same path as an Air Israel plane that was scheduled to leave five minutes before it, but the Air Israel flight was delayed, making TWA the first one over that area."

"So the terrorists thought they were taking down a flight to Israel? Instead they got TWA's flight to Europe?"

"How about that, Henry. Pretty interesting, huh?"

Henry was blown away by this whole concept. His nature made him skeptical of the possibilities, yet everything seemed to make sense. The terrorist "nation" was well known to be anti-Israel, so Jim's story seemed very plausible. Still, Henry barely knew him and couldn't be sure he wasn't being deceived. Maybe Jim was simply trying to impress him. He couldn't prove Jim was wrong, so maybe it was just Jim's way of trying to establish himself with Henry. With this mindset, Henry pressed on.

"Yeah, but that doesn't explain why it's such a secret. Why not say we caught the scum that did this and they're gonna pay? Why all the bullshit about it being some kind of pilot error or mechanical problem?"

"C'mon, Henry, think about it. It's August in an election year. How would it look to voters if three months before it's time to pick the leader of our country we were under terrorist attacks—one where innocent people were being killed in our own backyard? This by a president who spent the last four years cutting military spending by billions, not to mention someone whose only military action was to avoid being drafted! That might cost someone a lot of votes, maybe even re-election."

Even as it all started to make sense to Henry, he still wondered aloud, "How the fuck are they going to keep this from getting out?"

"I don't know just yet, Henry, but I'm gonna enjoy watching it as it develops. And remember, Henry, even though I work for you, if so much as one word leaves this office, my pipeline is severed."

"You mean *our* pipeline, don't you?" Then Henry smiled, as if he had just suckered another employee into buying one of his worthless partnerships. As Jim left his office, Henry yelled out to him, "Keep me up on this, Jim".

From that point on, every time Henry saw Jack Konnor give one of his press conferences he laughed as the FBI boss tried to sell the nation on his newest theories. Some people may have bought it, but Henry knew the truth, so he smiled and shook his head. It was a rush for him to have information that only a handful of people in the world had. Jim had already earned every penny paid to him, just for that alone. During the investigation, Jim constantly kept Henry up on all the little inaccuracies of the case. The most intriguing was the hiring of a retired forensic specialist, Dr. Robert Sli, to do the autopsies on some of the bodies recovered that night. Dr. Sli had been the leading forensic specialist used by the government for fifteen years before he retired to Charlotte, North Carolina in 1992. He was brought in to do autopsies on a handful of the victims. These were the bodies of those directly hit when the missile struck the plane, causing an implosion on certain parts of their bodies. If the plane had exploded from the fuel sparking, they would not show trauma inward, but outward. When Dr. Sli's reports confirmed this, there would be no way to continue with the mechanical error theory. However, by hiring an outsider who was long retired, they could simply cover up any reports contrary to the company line. They paid him a large fee for reports virtually no one would see; they couldn't. Those reports could conclusively show victims who sustained damage that could only be explained by something entering into the plane. By all accounts of the FBI, that was impossible if the plane had ignited, as they had stated. Despite overwhelming evidence of foul play, Sli's reports, as expected, were sealed and destroyed. As for Dr. Sli, he was sent back to the golf courses of North Carolina. It all seemed amazing to Henry, but he loved every bit of it.

When it was officially declared a mechanical error little over one year later, in September of 1997, Henry summoned Jim to his office. He had to get some answers. His curiosity got the best of him. Jim barely got into Henry's office before the grilling began. "How are they doing this? So many people have to know. Why are they still insisting it's mechanical?"

Jim could see that Henry was really questioning whether Jim had bull-shitted him about the whole thing.

"I mean, c'mon, why keep it a secret? The president was re-elected. What could be the reason?"

"Because, Henry, the people don't need to know, that's why. You, of all people, should understand that!"

After reflecting for a minute, Henry looked up at Jim. He knew exactly what Jim meant. He ran his company in a similar manner, always feeling no reason to let his employees in on what was happening within the framework of his firm. It was starting to make sense, at least to someone like Henry.

"But how do you orchestrate such deception?" Henry pressed on.

"All you need, Henry, is the top guys. The others aren't informed enough to prove anything."

"This, of course, meant getting to the top FBI agent in the state! If it got out, surely he would take the fall. Why should he go along, even if the president himself, asks?"

That question Jim had no answer for, at least not right away, but it wouldn't be long before Henry got that answer himself.

Shortly after the case of flight 800 was settled, Konnor retired from the FBI to take a job in the private sector. It seems he was offered a prestigious position in a large aviation company with an annual salary of $500,000; three times as much as what he made at the bureau. Coincidentally, it was a company with several government contracts that had made large contributions to the re-election of the president. Now every move made sense as to what Jim had told Henry.

"Still, what about the witnesses?"

"What witnesses?" Jim went on. "They were all sent home that night and never spoken to again. Who is gonna listen to them now, over a year later?"

"So that's how the story ends?" Henry wondered aloud.

"It's that simple…" Jim explained, "An accident occurred, the plane is taken apart, witnesses suppressed, and the president is re-elected. The country doesn't really want it to be a terrorist attack. That might disrupt their lives, put them in a state of fear. They want to continue living in their safe and sound world, even if it is a lie, so it's easier for most of them to just believe what they are told. The only guy who can prove anything is offered the job of a lifetime to keep it to himself, and yes, that's how the story ends."

Henry was both intrigued and amazed. It was mind-boggling that in this day and age such a deception could take place. It made him wonder what other events over the years had been covered up.

Henry left early that day, as he had more important issues to attend to. His daughter was sick with a high fever. He went home to be with her after picking her up a stuffed animal. Courtney Elizabeth had been born a year earlier in one of the very few events to bring Henry Larson to a state of tears. He was truly tough and ruthless in business, but his daughter was the one person who could render him weak. Not even his wife could do that. Every night Henry would spend at least an hour playing with her. He was not nearly as close to his son, Henry Jr., who spent more time with their nanny. When Henry got home, Courtney was always the focus of most of his attention.

# CHAPTER 6

▼

# UNEXPECTED CHRISTMAS PRESENTS

Christmas parties thrown by Catalano & Feinberg Securities were always the event of the season on Wall Street. Ben Catalano always spent an enormous amount of money as an expression of thanks to both his employees and customers. Although Ben was considered a tough businessman, he was always appreciative and liked to show it. This was the one time of year he let his hair down with his people. He always began the event by toasting first his clients, and then his employees. There wasn't a customer on Wall Street that didn't look forward to one of his parties. This was a tradition Henry didn't want to mess with. Although his motive wasn't really one of thanks, as Ben's was, it was more of an obligation to customers. Regardless, the Christmas party of 1999 was going to be the most magnificent ever, but this particular year Henry had a much different agenda. Since he intended to replace brokers with machines, Henry felt he needed to throw the biggest Christmas bash ever. He paid to have the Waldorf Astoria Hotel clear out all of its ballrooms for the event. He even hired Tony Bennett for $100,000 to sing for 45 minutes. The menu for the night included shrimp cocktail, lobsters and the finest steaks. Then there was the wine. Thousands of dollars of the finest wines from California to France were brought in. It appeared more like a political fund-raiser than a Christmas Party. Henry planned to shake lots of hands. He hoped this would at least soften customers to his idea of replacing some of their brokers. Things went as smooth that night as Henry could have possibly imagined. His employees were happy and his customers impressed. All things were going as scheduled.

About half way through the party, Henry came across a young woman who was eager to make his acquaintance. Samantha O'Hara was a 23-year-old Catalano employee. She had come to the firm only months after graduating from St. John's University the previous year. She was toiling in Catalano's operations area, waiting for her big break, but after a year she had become impatient. She saw this as an opportunity to impress Henry, and more importantly to get him to acknowledge her mere existence. Since they had both graduated from St. John's, Samantha felt that might be a door opener for their conversation. As she strolled toward him, his eyes couldn't help but fixate on her. She was a stunning, petite woman, five foot one, long brown hair, big green eyes and a killer figure. At first Henry thought she was a client, and was equally eager to meet her. Very few employees had the moxy to approach Henry so freely. Samantha introduced herself and struck up a conversation. They shared stories of St. John's University and courses their lives had taken while there—all the bullshit small talk one would expect of such a conversation. Eventually Henry asked her the dreaded question.

"So whom do you work for?"

Samantha nervously told him she was one of his employees. She jabbered away, hoping to keep the conversation alive, but it only took a few minutes before Henry had realized she was just another employee looking to get ahead. Despite her looks and his obvious attraction, he cooled to her. She had spent the last few minutes basically giving him her resume. This no longer interested him, and he cut her short.

"Look…Samantha, is it?" She nodded. "A lot of people with your qualifications are in the same boat as you. Nobody's willing to work any more to get ahead; they think it's owed to them." She tried to interrupt, but Henry wouldn't have any of it. "Listen, you want to move up in the firm? Go for the brass ring. Don't sit around waiting for someone to hand it to you. Now if you'll excuse me…"

Just like that, Henry was gone, but he had not seen the last of Samantha O'Hara that night. She was not taking "no" for an answer, even if it meant getting fired. She stewed for a while, and then took another shot at Henry. This time she was determined to achieve success. Henry once again dismissed her.

Several times, as she tried to approach him that night, Henry spotted her and turned away, starting conversations so as not to have to speak with her. So she waited. Later on, when Henry went to the men's room, Samantha waited about ten seconds and then burst into the bathroom, knowing Henry would be in a position where he couldn't walk away or ignore her. As she approached him, he looked up, rolling his eyes.

"Do you know where you are?" he asked.

Unfazed, she waited as the only other male left the bathroom. "Look here, Mr. Larson. I thought about what you said, and you're wrong. For the past year I did everything asked of me in my job. I am the first in every morning and the last to leave. I go above and beyond what is asked of me, but you're too arrogant to look as low as the operations area, so no matter what I do or how hard I work, I'll rot down there."

As she spoke, Henry finished and calmly zipped up his pants. He laughed and shook his head.

"Well, I'll give you credit; you're relentless. A pain in the ass, but relentless."

Samantha, undaunted, continued on. "I'm relentless, all right, but I'm not some dumb Jersey girl who chews gum and twirls her hair. I went to the same school as you and graduated with the same degree. All I ever asked for was the same chance you got."

Henry didn't know what to say. He liked the fire in her. She lit up, and he could not help but be a little attracted by it. Maybe it was all the wine he had drunk that night, or just an attraction he could no longer fight. Perhaps both. By that time it didn't matter. When she finally stopped, he leaned toward her. Henry grabbed her hair and began kissing her. Although she resisted at first, within seconds she was reciprocating. She seemed just as turned on as he was, and backed him into the handicapped stall of the men's room. Within seconds their tongues were dancing in each other's mouths. For a moment she pulled away from him, staring into his eyes. Henry wasn't sure what was happening. Just then he felt her hand rubbing against him. Henry's hands found their way to her breasts, and he began massaging them. After a few seconds, Samantha slowly made her way down to her knees, while looking up at Henry. She slowly unbuckled his belt, while reaching into his pants. Henry was clearly excited by this point, and Samantha smiled up at him. She massaged him before taking him into her mouth. Henry fell back against the door of the stall and his knees buckled as Samantha continued. He had never done anything like this before. He had met and married his wife Kate in college. They had a very conservative sex life. Never would it be conceivable that Kate would perform a sexual act in a men's room stall or any other place besides their bedroom; not that this had ever entered Henry's mind until now. This was entirely new and exciting to him. Samantha continued for a few minutes, until Henry climaxed. Once again, she looked up at him and they both smiled. Henry was breathing rapidly, trying to regain his composure as she slowly buckled his pants for him, then she rose to look him in the eye. Without saying a word, she had gotten her message across. She had made an impression, all right. This was some way to do it, he thought.

"I'm willing to do whatever I have to do to be noticed," she reiterated.

By now Henry was a bit uncomfortable. Someone else had come into the bathroom and entered the stall just two doors away from them. Henry could hear the loud sound of sniffing and he knew what was happening. He feared someone might come in and see them. He told Samantha to wait a few seconds before leaving their little handicapped love nest, and he quickly left the bathroom before the coke-snorting brokers left their stalls.

Normally Henry would wait to see who the guilty party was, but he felt for sure they heard what was going on in that handicapped stall, and the thought of being caught now frightened him to death. Most Wall Street guys wouldn't care, some even preferring to be seen so as to feed the "macho" Wall Street image, but for Henry it was a sign of weakness and something that could be a source of embarrassment, or worse, blackmail. That was the end of the night for Henry. Still feeling uncomfortable, he decided against rejoining the party. He made his way outside and found his driver. "Mohammed, get me home."

As instructed, Samantha waited several seconds before rejoining the party. She kept looking around for Henry, not knowing he had left. When she couldn't find him, she figured he was pissed. "Why else would he take off?" she wondered. She continued looking around for the better part of an hour before resigning herself to the fact that he had indeed gone. She dreaded going back to work on Monday.

The weekend went by quickly for Samantha. As she made her way into work on Monday, she wasn't sure what to expect: flowers, a call or a pink slip. With Henry, anything was possible. By lunchtime, when no flowers or a call came, she expected the worst. She spent the last several hours pacing around Catalano's Operations area. Several times her boss, Jimmy, asked her if everything was okay. She simply smiled and said, "Fine, Jimmy, fine." The day ended, and nothing had happened. Samantha would have to wait another day for her fate. She wondered what twisted game Henry was playing. He certainly wasn't drunk enough to forget what had happened. Was he just waiting a few days before getting rid of her to make it look good? The suspense was killing her. Maybe she should just quit. When she got in early Tuesday morning, her boss, Jimmy Speyer, called her into his office.

"Samantha, I got a call this morning." Samantha looked down, thinking, here we go, this is it. Then came her surprise. "Samantha, you're being moved. They're moving you to the options desk. You start today." Samantha couldn't help but fight back a smile. She thought for sure she was being fired. Never did she figure on a promotion. I guess she got to Henry after all. She hugged Jimmy and said goodbye to all the other back office workers. They were all happy for her. It was like an orphan being adopted. They all wanted to be the one, but they were glad that at least someone was moving up. It gave them all hope for themselves. Little did anyone know the price she had paid for this promotion.

When she arrived at her new desk, there were a dozen long-stem red roses waiting for her. It took Henry an extra day, but he had come through with flying colors. Although the note on the flowers simply said, "go for the brass ring," Samantha knew just where they came from.

That afternoon Samantha received a call from Henry, congratulating her on the promotion.

"I checked on you. Your work was exceptional according to Jimmy Speyer, so you're getting a shot here. I guess it can't be said that all Catalano employees don't have a chance to succeed here. Make the best of it."

Samantha wasn't sure if that was true or if Henry was trying to hide his real motive for the move. She didn't care. Either way, she was where she wanted to be.

"Can I buy you a drink tonight, Henry?"

"No, no, I don't think that's going to happen."

"Oh, okay I guess…" was all Samantha could get out before Henry interrupted her.

"No, tonight I'm busy…but Wednesday, say 7:00 pm at Il Tinellos might work."

"Il Tinellos? Where's that?" she asked.

"I'm sure someone with your resources will find it. See you then?"

Samantha hesitated for just a second before answering, "Yes, you will."

The phone clicked and Henry was gone. He cautiously looked forward to his rendezvous on Wednesday night.

Il Tinello Restaurant was an upscale Italian restaurant on 47th Street, far from the usual watering holes of the Catalano employees. Henry wanted to be certain he picked a place that was unlikely to include any acquaintances. He had dined there three or four times and never encountered a single person he knew. Besides, it was not like he had experience at this sort of thing. This was the best he could come up with on such short notice.

At 7:00 pm on Wednesday Henry nervously sat at the bar of Il Tinello Restaurant. He had been there since 6:30, rehearsing what he might say. He calmed himself with a double shot of Kettle One and club soda. His palms were still sweating as, right on schedule, Samantha walked through the door, looking more beautiful than he remembered her from the party. This time she was wearing a huge smile. How beautiful her smile was, Henry thought. They had a glass of white wine at the bar before being seated. Henry made sure he had reserved a table in the far corner of the restaurant. He wanted to be as secluded as possible.

Over the next few hours the two dined on pasta and drank several glasses of wine. Amazingly, very little of the conversation was business. Samantha had lots of questions about Henry, and she hung on his every word. Henry didn't know if it was the wine or the extra attention, but by dinner's end he felt very relaxed. He had a limousine waiting outside to drive Samantha home. All of this was mind-boggling to a girl who grew up in the middle of New Jersey. Here was this executive of one of the most successful brokerage firms in the world, with his two thousand dollar silk suit and private limo, having dinner with this little small-town Jersey girl. She couldn't explain it, but it sure felt right.

When they arrived at Samantha's apartment, she invited Henry up for a nightcap. As they made their way up the three-story walk, Henry looked around him, wondering what the hell he was doing in this God-awful place. He should have gotten a hotel room, he thought. Here he was, the CEO of one of the largest firms in New York, walking up three flights of stairs in what resembled a back alleyway when he should be opening the door to a suite in the Waldorf, but it was too late. They were already at her door.

As they walked into a small one-bedroom apartment, Henry looked around the living room and tiny kitchen. His only thought was how could someone live in a dump like this? It was smaller than his office!

"Whattya think, Henry? I know it's not much."

"No, it's, uh…nice. Kinda reminds me of my first apartment." At that point Henry felt obligated to lie to her. After all, they were about to sleep together, so he didn't want to say what he really felt, which was *let's get the hell out of here and go get a hotel room.* Needless to say, that was the last time Henry set foot in that apartment. Samantha and Henry spent the next several hours making passionate love. This was much different for Henry. Samantha was much wilder and more adventurous than he had ever experienced. It was a complete turn-on for him. About 2:00 a.m. Henry, exhausted, dragged himself from Samantha's bed.

"Where are you going?" she asked.

"Gotta go; I can't stay here. You know my situation."

"No I don't. What is your situation, Henry?"

"Hey, Samantha, I like spending time with you. It's nice to spend time together and I enjoy your company, but that's all this can be. If you can't handle that, tell me now."

Samantha felt the same way. She wasn't looking for anything long-term, and certainly not anything with a commitment. Her career was about to take off and that could only cause problems. She wanted to see if she could gain the upper hand in the relationship, but Henry made sure that wouldn't happen. She was no longer dealing with the local blue-collar Jersey boys she was used to dating. In all those relationships, she gained the upper hand until she had enough of them. Then she would dust them off or cast them aside for the next. No, Henry was no little Jersey boy. She liked that. What could she do but agree with him? After all, she had just gotten the promotion she was looking for. She certainly didn't want to jeopardize that.

"No, I'm fine with that. I had a good time tonight. When can I see you again?"

Henry stopped getting dressed for a moment and turned toward Samantha, who was sitting up in her bed. He looked at her beautiful naked body and then directly into her eyes. He wouldn't admit it to her, but he did like her. It was more than just letting off steam; he truly liked her.

"I usually work late on Wednesdays. Why don't we meet next Wednesday, same time and place? If you can't make it, don't call me."

"Then how can I get in touch with you?"

"You don't. If you're not there by 7:45 I'll assume you couldn't make it. In the same manner, if I am not there by 7:45, I won't be there. Just understand there can be no communication between us at the office right now."

Samantha thought this was bizarre. How paranoid could he be? Was she committed to this date? She couldn't not show up and make him go there and wait. She feared for her job too much. She was learning quickly just how much of a control freak Henry was. But what choice did she have? She did have a good time. He was even better in bed than she thought he would be, so why not?

"Okay, Henry. I look forward to it."

Minutes later, Henry kissed Samantha good-bye and took off. As he got into his waiting limousine and pulled away, he made a vow to himself. He never wanted to spend another minute in that apartment. The next morning Henry reserved a room for the following Wednesday at the Plaza Hotel, in the company's name.

This was just the beginning for Samantha and Henry. They began seeing each other on a regular basis. Wednesday was their night. Whether it was dinner at a fancy restaurant or a Broadway show or just a trip to the Plaza, it didn't matter. Of course Henry insisted they meet in obscure restaurants that were not frequented by Wall-Streeters. It started off as an innocent affair. For Henry, it was the thrill he had never had before. He was not very popular or good-looking, so for someone like Samantha O'Hara to want to be with him was exciting. Both were getting what they wanted out of the relationship: Henry, the thrill and Samantha, the opportunity.

That routine went on for years. To them it seemed the perfect relationship. Henry was getting much-needed attention, while Samantha's career was blossoming. No longer did she have to live in squalor in that apartment. Within a year she moved to a spacious two-bedroom apartment on 77th and Park Avenue. As much as Samantha wanted to move closer to downtown, Henry persuaded her that living uptown was a safer proposition—for him, of course.

Now they could spend time at her apartment where there was no chance of someone innocently stumbling into a bar or restaurant and spotting them. No more checking into hotels for one night without luggage, getting funny looks from bellmen and desk clerks. When Henry took the occasional business trip to Los Angeles or London, Samantha would often take a vacation and meet him there. This gave them several days together, away from their usual hidden relationship. While away, they could be a couple, go places together, and hold hands, whatever. They were getting a little closer than Henry wanted, but he couldn't stop; he liked her too much. Both seemed quite content with the situation.

Meanwhile, it was business as usual at Catalano Securities. It was 1999 and this was the year leading up to the new millennium. While the rest of the world feared all kinds of computer failure fueled by continuous rumors, Henry was busy driving forward in the final testing stages of his new trading system. It was a tense atmosphere around the office as whispers started that this would be the beginning of the end for brokering, as they knew it. Many Catalano employees knew the inevitable was near as they saw Glen Larson lurking around more and more.

The firm spent most of 1999 soliciting its customers to put their system on their respective trading desks. They were met with some resistance, as traders realized a lot of their brokers who had become friends and confidants could lose their jobs. This pissed Henry off. He hated the brokers even more and blamed them for the resistance his customers showed toward him and his system. So, he called for a meeting. He met each department separately, but the message was the same to each of them. He flat-out accused them of a conspiracy to stop the installation of his system. He tried to appeal to them and threaten them at the same time, as only Henry could do.

"You people are keeping this firm from growing. We know some of you told your customers not to take the system. What you don't realize is that if it's not us, it's going to be someone else. By us being first you can have job security. If some other firm beats us to the punch, we'll all be out in the street."

Henry was very believable, except to the ardent Larson haters who by now knew to believe nothing that came from his mouth. After all, isn't this the same guy that a few years ago graciously sold worthless partnerships to most of them? Now they're supposed to buy this! The problem was that some of them needed to believe him because they had very few options left. Ultimately, they were left with no choice. Eventually Henry wore them down, and they bought it. As for the others, Henry needed more to convince them.

"For those of you who don't promote the system, you will be considered insubordinates. That's grounds for dismissal and cause for forfeiting your partnerships. You'll lose your jobs and your money."

The brokers sat there, somewhat stunned. How many times was this one agreement going to come back to haunt them? On one hand, Henry was assuring his people that going along with the program would be financially beneficial to them. On the other was the threat of unemployment and possible legal action. What choice did they have but to hope it worked out?

With the brokers reluctantly assisting Catalano's customers, one by one they agreed to have Henry's trading system installed at their trading desks, but there were some problems Henry didn't foresee. Conforming the new trading system with customers' current computer information bases became somewhat of a problem. The system was designed to conform to a basic software program. However, some clients had deviated to systems much more complex. Therefore, Henry's computer "wiz kids" now had to write a program that would make it possible and workable to interface into their customers' complex software. This delayed the completion of installation into customers by more than six months, but with the help and cooperation of the brokers, all the customers were ready to go by Labor Day of 2000. It was at that point Henry was to drop yet another bombshell on his partners.

Henry announced the formation of a new company called "Rapid Trading". Rapid Trading would be the name of this new electronic trading system. The big news in the announcement was that "Rapid Trading" would act as a totally separate company and entity from Catalano & Feinberg. This meant the partners of Catalano had no stake whatsoever in Rapid Trading or its profits! Desk heads and senior brokers were incensed at this announcement. That night they secretly met at the Tall Ships to discuss what the hell had just happened to them. How could it be possible that a system that was built with profits and partnership money that they provided could be considered a separate company? It was mind-boggling—something only a little shit like Henry could conjure up. Several hours later, after engulfing massive amounts of alcohol at the Tall Ships, some very drunk brokers had come to an agreement. This time they would fight back. They would no longer lie down while Henry fucked them. This time they would bond together. After discussing their options for several hours, they decided they would sue.

"Larson's not getting away with it this time." With that Gary Short raised his bottle of Heineken to toast the united group, most of whom by that time could barely comprehend anything being said. Of course there were some who had a more simple solution: kicking Henry's ass all over Wall Street. Most of the brokers actually preferred that over potential litigation, especially knowing that a legal fight meant having to go to battle with one of the dirtiest fighters they'd ever encountered.

But Henry was a full step ahead of his employees. Before they even had the pleasure of telling Larson of their decision to sue him, he called a meeting of all desk heads. Henry knew that as much as he did not respect these brokers, they were capable of hurting him. He was well armed with a plan when the meeting started.

"I guess I surprised a few of you the other day with our announcement of Rapid Trading. I didn't have a chance to set any of you down until now to explain. This move—creating a new company—was necessary to protect all of the partners. We structured Rapid Trading so that the partners, and only the partners, would share in the profits."

Short, who was seething in the back of the room, could not hold his anger and shouted, "Maybe I'm stupid, but how is that going to work if it's a separate company?"

This prompted several other employees to murmur "Yeah, how about it, Henry?" Henry was unfazed by their anger and continued. "Glen is heading up this venture, so I felt it appropriate for him to address you all today. Glen…" At that point Glen Larson stepped up from his chair and took center stage. This was the first time he had ever addressed the partners. He looked nervous as he fumbled around for the few notes he had written down. Finally, after what seemed like an eternity, Glen spoke.

"Henry decided that the only way you partners would be compensated for the success of the electronic trading company was to form this company—a separate company from Catalano—and offer all Catalano partners stock options. This structure ensures that you, the partners and the backbone of our business, will receive what is rightfully yours. By offering all of you stock options, it prevents other employees who were not Catalano partners from drawing from the profits, thus draining money from all of your pockets!"

For a moment there was silence. Once again skepticism filled the air, as it did whenever a Larson spoke. The managers all looked at each other, some whispering doubts, others just waiting to see how they could get fucked in this new deal. It seemed that Glen Larson had some of the same talent as his big brother: lying with such conviction that even skeptics eventually believed him. The brilliant move here was that all of this wasn't coming from Henry, but from Glen. Henry knew the partners would not believe anything he brought them. He had screwed them all too many times. He needed a new messenger to deliver his next lie. That's where Glen came in.

Glen went on to explain that now, more than ever; they needed to push their customers to use Rapid Trading.

"The quicker our customers adapt, the faster you guys get rich."

He also told them that within six months the plan was to bring Rapid Trading public, and then the IPO (initial public offering) would be as high as $35 per share! Their options would be at a mere $25 per share, which would represent a 40% profit should the IPO price be correct. He then outlined the guidelines for the options. Brokers would have three years to exercise their options, but could not do so in the first year.

"The stock should hit 100 by then," was Glen's proclamation. "Every partner at the meeting should fully expect to cash in big with Rapid Trading. This was the one way you all could be paid back for all your patience and support during the building and development of this state-of-the-art trading system. Your just reward is now at your fingertips."

As the meeting concluded, the partners cautiously congratulated each other once they were outside. Glen was a huge hit, and his sincerity had almost all of them believing that somehow he had gotten to his brother and righted the ship. As the brokers mingled away from the conference rooms, they began high-fiving each other. At the same time, Glen and Henry were celebrating in Henry's office.

"You were awesome, Glen. Even I believed that shit about the stock going to 100!"

"Well, I can't take all the credit, Henry. After all, I learned from the best—...you!"

"Did you ever think you would see a group as gullible as this, Glen? I mean, where else could you fuck someone over and over again and have them beg you for more?" They both laughed for a while before doing some high-fiving of their own.

# CHAPTER 7

▼

# BYE-BYE BROKERS

By the end of the year 2000, Rapid Trading was in full swing. Although business was booming overseas, it was sluggish in the United States. While small institutions were on board, the primary dealers—those clients covered by the brokers—had not yet participated. Still, everything was in position for Henry to move forward. Henry and Glen's grand plan called for a pilot phase, or trial period. This meant that traders for three months would agree to only trade using the Rapid Trading system, not using Catalano Securities or their brokers at all! Of course the brokers were assured that this was just a trial and they were to support the move with their clients or, once again, face the wrath of Henry.

Since it was just a trial, Henry and Glen decided to experiment with one department to see how the brokers and their clients would react. Henry assured all the employees that no one would lose their jobs unless they spoke negatively against the system. The department Henry selected was futures trading. For members of that desk, being selected was, to them, the reverse of winning the lottery. When told they were chosen for this very important test, every broker expressed a feeling like "a lamb being led to the slaughter." They knew that if the test was successful, Henry, for sure, would either fire them or cut their salaries to the point where they might as well quit anyway, and Henry was preparing to do just that. His plan was to cut salaries 50% across the board. He would do this, knowing that a fair amount of employees would quit immediately. Those who stayed would make so little money it wouldn't matter. Either way, the move would reduce salary overhead by probably 60% to 75%. As much as he would rather fire all of them, Henry still feared backlash from clients. He figured giving his partners inflated stock options might show the customers he was not trying to screw them, except by now employees and customers assumed the worst.

It was Monday, February 3$^{rd}$ of 2001, when the trial period for Rapid Trading began. The brokers all strolled in as if it were any other Monday. It was anything but that. There was nothing for them to do that day but watch their screens. Some played on their computers or shuffled cards, while others read newspapers. There was the occasional joke when the phone rang, but today the only voices on the other side were friends and family members—not clients. Henry sat in his office, calmly waiting for his brother Glen to bring him updates as the day progressed. It was at this time that Eddie Macanee slammed a hundred-dollar bill down on his desk. "Ben Franklin here says none of my customers are the first trade." This typical group of Wall Street brokers was followed by a frenzy of betting on whose account would be the "Judas" and cave in first. Bets were posted on an easel board. If your customer did a trade, you were out. The last customer not to trade would represent the winner and his broker would take home the whole pot. At least now the brokers had something to occupy their time. They anxiously watched to see which account would be first to post a trade and thus be eliminated. Who would be the first to drive the sword of destiny into their very existence as brokers? To their amazement, by 10:00 am there was no loser yet. Not one trade in the first hour.

"Well, we all still have jobs, I guess," one broker nervously joked.

At 11:00 am there was still nothing. By this time you could cut the tension in the room with a knife. The clock moved so slowly that minutes seemed like hours. Here were twenty experienced brokers with an average of twelve years experience, as nervous as their first day of work. Now it was 2:00 pm, and it was Henry who was feeling the pressure more than his brokers. No one had given in yet. Not one trade. How was this possible? Henry had Glen check to make sure everyone's system was working. He could not comprehend what was happening. How could they go six hours without doing a single trade? On a normal day the futures area would do between two hundred to two hundred and fifty trades, which represented twenty-five trades an hour yet they were six hours in and nothing! Henry was rapidly losing his patience. As 5:00 pm approached, there was still nothing. Once again Macanee stood on his desk. This time he looked at all his co-workers and began clapping. One by one, every broker stood and joined in applauding their accounts. This went on for several minutes, while brokers slapped each other's hands in triumph as other areas stood to see the commotion.

By now the word had spread, and they too joined in. The trading day was over and not so much as one trade was printed on the futures desk with their accounts. It was their customers that would ultimately do for the brokers of Catalano Securities what they could not do for themselves. They were sending a message, loud and clear, to Henry Larson. "Don't fuck with our friends, our brokers."

Seemingly unfazed, Henry came in the next day as if nothing had happened, and the experiment continued, but once again Henry experienced failure.

This went on for a full week. Customers did not bend. They did not flinch in their resolve. In the end, it was Henry that would angrily call off the trial—Immediately—after which business miraculously returned. As much as it killed him to admit it, Henry knew his business was still too dependent on his "dime-a-dozen" order takers: his brokers. Needless to say, this infuriated Henry. His perfect plan was not only set back, but seemingly destroyed! Within a few months, he planned to be rid of most of these brokers and now he was stuck with them unless he could figure out a way to get their customers on his side. Much to Henry's chagrin, he had no plan for that, at least not yet. It was a complete victory for the employees of Catalano Securities. For the first time, they had defeated Henry Larson. Or should it be said, their clients did. Either way, they had something to celebrate for the first time in years. Their traders stonewalled Henry's attempt at electronic trading and they were all back at their positions, seemingly once again comfortable that their jobs were safe, at least for now. Rapid Trading would have to succeed without the help of the Street's largest customers. Of course Henry knew this was not possible. Sure, it could make money, but he hadn't spent five years and one hundred million dollars to make "a little money." No matter how long it took, Henry promised to persevere until every major dealer was actively using his system. But for now he had to swallow his pride for another day.

In the summer of 2001, Rapid Trading stock went public, as promised by Glen Larson. It opened at $35 a share and quickly rose to $50 per share. This was strongly due to very little trading volume and Henry bidding up the stock each day. This was safe, he thought. After all, who was going to sell it to him? The partners had to wait a year, so no one had the stock except the ones who bought when it went public. He met little resistance while he moved the stock to $50 per share. Henry and Glen made sure to point this out to employees as often as possible. But what good was it? No one could profit by exercising their options for a year. It didn't take long for Wall Street analysts to realize that the stock was extremely over-valued and trading much higher than the company's worth. It was not reviewed favorably, and by the end of August 2001, less than two months after the stock first opened, the price of the stock dropped dramatically. It was now trading at $8 per share, far from the original $35 or close to the $25 stock options owned by the partners. Now, once again, the partners were shaking their heads as they realized that by using his brother Glen, Henry had once again gotten the best of them. What the partners never knew was that there was no restriction on Henry's shares and he sold most of his stock between $40 and $50 per share,—not the highest it traded, but well above what it was before it had lost its luster and fell like a stone in a pond. Then he simply bought it all back, between eight and ten dollars. As Henry himself owned 100,000 shares, this was a profit of over two million dollars. Not a bad take for two months' work. This was a rebound for Henry's loss to the brokers in February. Still, he had not moved any closer to reaching his goal of eliminating his brokers while he converted his business to his machines. His feelings had only grown stronger in the past months, never wavering in his opinion of how useless he felt they all were to him. However, he had no plan as to how he could make this happen. Little did he know that this problem was only a few weeks away from solving itself.

# CHAPTER 8

▼

# SAVING HENRY

**Sunday, September 9, 2001, 8:30 am.**

Jim Swimhammer telephoned Henry Larson at home. He asked to meet with him.

"Jesus, Jim, its Sunday! Why the hell are you bothering me?"

Jim sounded nervous as he spoke. "Henry, I really need to see you right away."

Despite some prodding by Henry, Jim refused to discuss what was bothering him over the telephone. Reluctantly, Henry agreed, and Jim made his way to Henry's door within the hour.

Henry offered Jim a cup of coffee and escorted him to the backyard. As they sat on Henry's patio, Jim slowly sipped his coffee, while staring out at Henry's estate. He couldn't help but notice the finely trimmed lawn, the glistening of the sun on the pool and the beautiful landscaping with colorful plants and trees.

"Its beautiful here, Henry. You're a lucky man. Look around at what you have here. Wife, kids, a house that most people could only dream about."

Henry by now had become impatient with Jim. He didn't know what was bothering him, but he sure didn't feel like listening to him give a play-by-play of his life.

"Jim, this better be fucking good. You took me away from a Sunday with my family. I know it's not to tell me how pretty you think my trees and plants are." Jim just stared at Henry. "What the hell is it? Jim, you're staring at me like you just saw the boogie man or something."

"My brother called me this morning. I thought it was to talk football. You know today is opening day for the Jets. We used to always go as kids. It was the one thing we looked forward to every year. But that's not what he wanted to talk about."

Henry put down his coffee and once again stared into Jim's eyes. "Jim, what is it?"

"We intercepted some messages, Henry."

"*We*, who's *we*?"

"We, the United States of America, that's who!" This whole discussion clearly was rattling Jim and making him uncomfortable.

"The messages we intercepted were from the Al Qaida; you know, Bin Laden."

"The terrorist?" This perked Henry right up.

"We intercepted some cell phone messages of him telling family members that he was going away. That in two days something would happen. Something big that would make the world, especially America, realize his power. Something that would require him to go into hiding for a long time."

Henry looked inquisitively at Jim. "And this couldn't wait until tomorrow?"

"Well, I just thought you would like to know, as he claimed to be targeting either DC or New York."

Once again this got Henry's attention. "What else do you know? I mean, what are the targets? Do they know?"

"In Washington it would be either..."

Henry interrupted. "I don't give a shit about Washington. They could blow the whole thing up and I couldn't care less. What about New York?"

"Well...either the United Nations or perhaps the World Trade Center."

Henry turned and slowly walked away from Jim. He didn't say a single word.

Jim went on. "They don't know how or what precautions to take yet, but they feel that they'll try, as they have in the past, during the morning rush hours. This is when there the most people—lots of congestion and confusion because most people aren't fully awake yet and are rushing to work."

Henry looked down, shaking his head side-to-side. Waiting another minute or so, he calmly responded to Jim,

"What else you can find out about this, Jim? I mean this is big. We need to know more."

"I don't know if I'm getting any more information than I already have. That's how it works. But I wanted you to know right away."

"Does anyone else know about this?"

"Are you crazy, Henry? I can't tell anyone this. You are the only one."

"Okay, Jim, calm down." Henry waited a minute and put a hand on Jim's shoulder, trying to calm him. "I gotta digest this whole thing, Jim. Go home, relax; you're too tense. Watch some football on T.V. Like you said, it's opening day. You're a Jet fan. Go watch the game. Let's meet tomorrow, say 8:00 am, in my office. We'll figure this thing out."

Jim didn't know what to say. He surely expected a different response from Henry. Henry seemed almost completely unaffected by news that could potentially translate into extreme danger to him and his company. Still, Jim took Henry's advice and spent the rest of the day staring at his T.V., but his focus was not on any games on that day. He kept thinking about the words his brother had told him. It's one thing when you hear about incidents that don't affect you. This, though, potentially was staring Jim right in the face.

Meanwhile, Henry immediately called his brother. "Glen, get over here, right away!"

Glen, being single, liked his Saturday nights out. He truly loved everything about the city life. On a typical Saturday night you would not find him back home until the early morning hours, so when Henry called Glen at the ungodly hour of 10:00 am, he naturally encountered an incoherent voice on the other end of the telephone.

"Who the hell is this?" Glen muttered.

"Glen, its Henry. I need you to come here immediately."

"Why, is somebody dead? If not, call me back in about twelve hours."

"Glen!" Henry screamed, "This is serious! Get up and come over here." Glen grunted before answering. "Okay, okay. I'll be right over."

Glen hung up the phone and rolled over in bed. He lay there for a few minutes before sitting up. Shit, I might as well get going or he'll call me every half hour, he thought to himself. Glen dragged himself out of bed and stumbled into the shower. The cold water was a rude awakening, but one he needed. He threw on a pair of jeans that were lying on the floor, put on a shirt, grabbed his jacket and was on his way. By the time Glen trekked from Manhattan out to Jersey, it was almost noon. By this time, Henry was nervously pacing around the house.

Kate let Glen in and greeted him with a kiss.

"What's up, Kate?"

"I don't know, Glen. Jim Swimhammer dropped by and Henry has been pacing around the yard since he left. He won't tell me anything. Says its nothing—work related—not for me to worry about. Maybe you can calm him down."

Glen smiled at his sister-in-law and gave her a hug. "You know Henry. Someone's probably undercutting his commissions or something like that. I'll take care of him." Kate smiled and walked Glen into the kitchen. Henry saw him and walked back into the house.

"Jesus, Glen. When I said to come over, I meant today!"

Glen ignored Henry and made himself at home, fixing himself a much-needed cup of coffee. While sipping it, he calmly inquired about what was so important that required him to be dragged from his bed, still very hung over from the night before.

"Come with me." Henry walked Glen into his office.

Henry explained, in detail to Glen, what Jim Swimhammer had just, a few hours earlier, relayed to him. This seemed to sober Glen up a little faster than the coffee. Glen looked at Henry with confusion.

"So what should we do, notify the board?"

Henry had no plans of sharing this information. "Glen, lets think about this for a second. We certainly can't tell everyone to stay home, now can we? I mean, realistically, the chances of a threat being successful, or even real, are about, what, a thousand to one, maybe higher? Besides, we're not supposed to even have this information. Do you know how much money we would lose closing down, not to mention throwing the people in the company—no, the whole fucking city— into a state of panic! Real or not, people are going to ask how and what we knew. That would blow all future information that might come our way."

Glen interrupted. "Henry, what's the use of having this information if you're going to ignore it?"

"I never said that, Glen." Henry paced around his office, looking very deep in thought. "No, I have other ideas." Henry, while still pacing in his office, turned toward Glen and continued. "Let's say that there is a 99% chance it's just a threat. They've already failed once at trying to hit our building, and our security is much tighter now than it was in '93. For them to sneak another bomb in would be almost impossible. Besides, they used a truckload last time, and that was a miserable failure. I think it's more likely they'll go for the UN or one of the buildings in DC, if at all. However, if our building is the target..." Henry stopped for a moment, nodding his head up and down "...if we are the target, it might solve a lot of our problems."

"How the hell would a bomb going off in the Trade Center help solve our problems, Henry?"

"Think about it, Glen. After the last attack, how many brokers were afraid and didn't want to come back?" Henry was, of course, referring to the 1993 bombing that still haunted his employees.

"A lot, Henry—like a third of them."

"Well, on the small chance that our building gets hit again, what do you think their reaction would be? It's been eight years since the '93 bombing. Most of the brokers make less money now, and they know if something happens we're still not moving out of that building. I think a bunch will quit and a bunch will try to end up on some kind of long-term disability. Either way, this leaves us with a lot less contracts to have to buy out to accelerate the growth of Rapid Trading."

"Yeah, great Henry, but what about the risk?"

Henry was like a little kid on Christmas morning. The more he spoke, it was like he was opening another present. "We're way up top. In '93 we had not one casualty. Not one! I think the risk is minimal. Besides, we've already agreed that we can't close the firm or tell people we even have this information. I mean, this is just a hypothetical, or a just-in-case scenario we're talking about here." Henry wasn't finished yet. Even though he had but a few hours to dream up this whole scheme, he seemed incredibly efficient.

"So as I see it, Glen, maybe Tuesday is a good day for you to call in sick."

"Oh...I see. And what about you, Henry?"

Just then, as Henry's wife Kate strolled by the office where Henry and Glen were talking, Henry yelled out to her "Honey, I think I'll take Courtney to school on Tuesday."

Somewhat in a state of shock, Kate stopped. She backed up and peered into the room where Henry and Glen were. "What's the occasion?" she asked.

"I need a reason to take my daughter to school now?"

"No, Henry. I'm just wondering why you never took Henry, Jr. to school."

"Well, I made a mistake there, and I don't want to make the same mistake with Courtney. It's time for me to get more involved with both of them."

"Okay," she said, "but Monday is her first day of school. Why not then? That's when most fathers show up."

That, however, did not fit into Henry's plan. "I wish I could, but I have a meeting I can't miss. I'll take her on Tuesday." Kate smirked before strolling away. She knew Henry was up to something. This was not in his nature to simply turn on the "I wanna be a good daddy" switch. But whatever his reason, she thought it was good for Courtney, so she didn't give it another thought. As for Henry, he turned to his brother and gestured as if to say it's as easy as that."

By this time Glen's wheels were turning as well. "I think it will look suspicious if we're both out that day, Henry, don't you?"

Henry agreed. "But how do we avoid that? I don't want you to be there, Glen, just in case. You're my only brother, and besides Kate and the kids, you're all the family I have in this world."

Glen rubbed his hands over his eyes and then looked up at Henry. "Okay, here's an idea. Tuesday I get into work early, say 7:30 am. I'll walk around, talk to a few people—you know, make sure I'm seen. But by 8:00 am I'll go out of the building for breakfast or something. Jim said the morning rush, right? The morning rush is like 8:00 to 9:00 am, right? If anything is going to happen, it will be no later than 10:00 am. So I'll come back around 11:00 am."

Henry smiled with approval. "Okay, but you need to be out before 8:00 am. That's too close for comfort. Like I said, I don't want you taking any chances. Matter of fact, the more I think about it, the more I don't like it." Henry paused for a minute before continuing. "Scrap it. I don't want you going there at all. It's just too risky."

"Henry," Glen started, "I know you're my big brother and you always try to take care of me, but I can take care of myself now. Let me do this. I'm a big boy; I can handle it. Henry, please..."

Henry paused. His every feeling told him to say no, but he knew Glen was right. He had to cut the umbilical cord sooner or later. He endorsed Glen's plan and gave him a long hug like a parent sending his kid off to camp or college for the first time.

The Larson boys were delighted with themselves. They actually felt, maybe even hoped, that an attack of some kind would occur. They had it all worked out. Henry even made sure another board member would be away from the building that morning. He needed to insure that a majority of board members be protected, just in case. He would send Rick Stein on a fictitious meeting uptown, never telling him of his true motive. The only three men who knew what was happening were Henry, Glen and Jim Swimhammer. That night Henry had trouble sleeping. He wasn't sure whether it was from fear or excitement. Either way, he was happy to see Monday morning roll around.

## 7:30 am, Monday, September 10th, 2001

Henry arrived at work. He exited his car, saying goodbye to Mohammed, his driver. As he walked toward the building, he took a second to look up at the towers. Except for his first day of work, he could never remember taking the time to look up and actually admire the beauty and stature of the majestic buildings. It was almost as if he were giving one long good look, just in case. He then proceeded, as he had for the last thirteen years, up the elevator to the 99th floor. He strolled into his office to ready himself for his 8:00 am meeting with Swimhammer, but Jim was already waiting for him.

"You're early, Jim. Any new news?" Henry closed the door behind him.

Jim shook his head, indicating "No." "I had a little trouble sleeping, so I came in early."

"Not me," lied Henry. "I slept like a baby. Why are you so nervous, Jim?"

"Shit, Henry, are you kidding? This is scary stuff. How do you just ignore it?"

Again, Henry reiterated, "Who said I'm ignoring it? I've considered what you said, but what should I do: close the company on a rumor, one that I'm not even supposed to know about? How long do you think it would take people in power to realize where my information came from, Jim, huh?"

Jim stared away. "So what do we do, Henry? Nothing?"

"I'm sending Rick Stein up to First Boston tomorrow morning. I want you to accompany him. Maybe between the two of you can find a way to soften their position on our rapid trading system."

"Soften their position! They fucking hate you, Henry! How do you soften that?"

"Just go with Rick. I set it up for 9:00 a.m., but be there at 8:30, okay?"

Just then it registered in Jim's head what Henry was doing. "And where will you be, in case I need to get in touch, back here at the office?"

"No! I'm taking my daughter to school. I probably won't make it in 'til 9:30 or 10:00 o'clock; it depends."

Jim didn't have to ask any more questions. He could clearly see what Henry was doing, and he was glad to be part of the few people Henry felt the need to protect. "What do we do now, Henry?"

Henry peered out the window, admiring the view of the city, never even turning to acknowledge Jim. "Just let me know if there's any new news." Jim waited a moment, realizing Henry was done with him, before going on his way.

After Henry and Jim had completed their meeting, Henry sat alone in his office. Staring blankly out his office window, he pondered all the possibilities of what might be—if, in fact, this information were true. What else could he do to prepare for this? Was he forgetting something? Then his thoughts turned to Samantha O'Hara, the woman he had shared many intimate nights with over the past few years. Now, as he reflected on those times, his true feelings were playing out in his mind. He couldn't just let her come to work. He had to do something to protect her. By now they weren't just lovers, but more. Sure, they still played the same game, like it was just a casual physical relationship, but how could it be? They had been seeing each other for almost three years. Although never asked to, Samantha had stopped dating other men for over a year and a half. Yes, they had been fighting as of late, but all couples do that. For the first time since that first day of their relationship, he picked up the phone and called down to her at her desk, not caring who might pick up the phone. When she picked up, she was stunned to hear Henry's voice.

"Samantha, can you come up to my office, please?"

She paused for a second before simply responding, "Sure".

As she slowly walked toward Henry's office, Samantha's mind thought the worst while playing terrible scenarios in her head. Was he firing me, or perhaps breaking it off? Just the week before, she had pressured him about their relationship. She had grown tired of the secret Wednesday nights and hiding their feelings. She told him she loved him. It wasn't supposed to happen, but it did. When Henry panicked, she never finished the conversation. She never got to tell him that she was pregnant with his baby. Now she felt sure he was about to break her heart. She slowly made her way across the trading floor to his office. She kept her head down; fearing people were staring at her.

When she finally arrived, Henry's door was open. As she knocked, she could see Henry rocking back and forth in his chair, facing toward the window.

"Come in, Samantha, and close the door."

Samantha closed the door slowly and turned toward Henry. Henry spun around in his chair, facing Samantha. He wasn't sure how to tell her.

"Samantha, I want you to understand that I care about you—a lot."

Samantha interrupted him. She figured she wanted him to know everything before he cast this final blow to her.

"Henry, I'm pregnant."

"What?"

"You heard me. I wanted to tell you last Wednesday, but you freaked out on me."

Henry covered his face with his hand and took a deep breath. This changes everything, he thought. It was no longer just an affair. This was now raised to a new level. A baby! He wasn't sure how to feel. I mean, in one respect he felt joy, but that was quickly overtaken by thoughts of fear. Now all he could think of was the scandal this could cause him. He looked up at Samantha. She was half smiling, half crying. What should he do?

"Samantha, this…this blows me away. When did you find out you were pregnant?"

"Just a week ago. I wanted to tell you, but you got upset when I told you how I felt, so I thought I would wait until you calmed down; now you're firing me."

"Firing you? No, no, I'm not…I mean, I would never do that."

Samantha took a moment to wipe her face. She looked into Henry's eyes. "Then why did you call me to your office, Henry? What is it?"

Henry was lost. He didn't know what direction to turn. Eventually his instincts just took over.

"There is so much to say, but not here, not now."

"When, Henry? When?" Tears were streaming down her face. She still wasn't sure if Henry was happy, sad, or mad about the news.

After a short pause, Henry determined her fate. He took another minute and in that time, every moment of their relationship passed before him: all the romantic dinners, passionate nights and trips around the world. For a second he choked on a feeling he didn't know how to deal with. Still, he found it within himself to do what came natural to him. He turned his answer into a business decision, as cold as any other he had made in the past.

"Tomorrow, Samantha. Let's have dinner tomorrow night. I promise we'll talk then."

Samantha nodded her head as she acknowledged Henry. She did her best to regain her composure before she headed back towards her desk. She left Henry's office and went to the ladies room to freshen up. Just like that, Henry made his decision not to tell Samantha. He didn't want scandal or divorce or a bastard child, so he would leave Samantha to be with everyone else. The fact that he loved her didn't matter; his image was more important.

For most of the day, business went on as usual. More than a few times Henry thought about calling Samantha back and telling her his real reason for summoning her to his office. A few times he even picked up the phone. Each time he put it back down. As much as he loved her, he didn't want to face the music. Not now, at least. If nothing happened, he would deal with it then.

Henry and Glen barely spoke to each other that day. Whenever their paths crossed, they simply nodded or winked at each other. Earlier that morning, Henry had whispered to Glen to meet him at 5:00 pm in his office. They agreed not to speak about any of this until then, and both kept true to their word.

Jim spent most of the day working the phones to see what new information he could acquire. It took several hours for him to get through to his brother, and when he did, his brother was short with him. "Not now, Jim. Stay close to your phone. I'll call you when I can." And that was it.

All the while, the rest of Catalano's employees experienced a normal Monday. No one could even conceive what potentially loomed over him or her. Jim had trouble even looking at them as they went about their business. Whether they were trading, going to the bathroom, or just having lunch, he couldn't help but wonder how they would react if they found out what he knew.

As the hours went by without any word, Jim became visibly nervous, pacing about, fiddling with paper and constantly looking at his watch.

At 4:15 pm, his waiting was over. The telephone rang. Jim answered his phone in the same manner he had every time he picked it up—"Jim Swimhammer"—with a stern tune to it. The voice on the other end was soft, but direct.

"Is this a taped line?" the voice asked.

"No," Jim answered.

"We intercepted more messages but have not been able to decode them yet. All we could get were cryptic statements. One was that tomorrow was 'the big match.' The other communication referred to September 11th as being 'zero hour.' There have been unusually high amounts of emails and phone calls today, fueling the speculation that this is real. The problem is, they communicate a lot in code over the Internet and change websites every other day, so tracking them sometimes takes longer than we would like."

Jim interrupted his brother. "So do you have any idea what the target might be?"

"Hell, Jim, we're not even sure it's real! Bin Laden seems to have disappeared as well. We think he's either in Afghanistan or Pakistan, but he has ceased communicating with anyone for the past 48 hours, so I'm not sure what to think. I'm just telling you, we're on high alert, and so is the FAA."

"The FAA?? When did that enter the equation? I mean, are they blowing up planes, or what?"

"Not sure, little brother. Just do what you can to protect yourself, and, don't call me anymore today, okay?"

"Okay, Ken. I hope I didn't cause you any problems with all the calls."

"No, it's okay. I just won't be able to talk to you until we figure this out."

Jim took a deep breath, exhaling slowly. "Can I call you tomorrow?"

"I hope you can, Jimmy. I hope you can."

With that, the phone went dead. Jim held the phone in his hands for several seconds while his mind absorbed what he had just heard. He called Henry and told him he had more news. Henry told him "5:00 pm, my office," and hung up.

By the time Glen arrived at Henry's office on Monday at 5:00 pm, Jim was already briefing him.

"I think this is real, Henry." Jim filled Henry in on his conversation with his brother, leaving out no details.

"The FAA?" Henry blurted.

"Yeah, I had the same reaction, Henry." By the time Jim had finished, all three of them feared there was real danger upon them. But Henry remained cool. He set Glen and Jim down and proceeded to outline a plan—the same way he outlined every plan, as if it was just another hurdle or bump in the road.

"Glen, I want you to get to work by 7:30 am. No, make it 7:15, and make sure you're seen! Then head downstairs. Make sure you're out by 7:45. Don't mess around Glen I'm serious. Get out of there. Take a cab to Jersey. Stay away from the trains just in case that's the target. Should something happen, no cell phone! Go to the coffee shop in the Newark train station. I'll meet you there around 8:30 am." Henry sounded like a general issuing orders during wartime. He was preparing as if an attack was imminent.

Then he turned to Jim. "Jim, remind Stein that you have the meeting uptown. Make sure he doesn't miss it and isn't late. I don't care if you have to go to his apartment and dress him in the morning. Make damn sure you're uptown by 8:30. As a matter of fact, I want you to pick him up. I don't intend to take any chances on him showing up here by mistake. That meeting won't last long, so make sure you are not here before 11:00 am. If something is going to happen, it will be early. Correct?"

"That's what they believe, Henry."

"Then 11:00 am should be safe. All right." He paused. "Well, it should be an interesting day tomorrow, huh?"

Henry, Glen and Jim stared around the room at each other. Neither Glen nor Jim had anything to say. Henry looked at Jim one final time.

"Go home and sleep. If you hear anything else, be sure to call me, no matter what time of night it is."

"What about you, Henry?" Jim asked.

"Oh, I'll be taking my little girl to school, meeting teachers and having breakfast. I'll see you around 11:00 am." Henry smiled and once again glared out his window, not even realizing fully that it would be the last time he would have that view.

Shortly after their meeting, Henry was on his way home as usual

Henry's driver, Mo, was waiting for him outside the Trade Center at 5:30 pm, as he had for the past four years, but this ride was not to be a normal one for Henry. He was anxious that night. One way or another, he couldn't wait for Tuesday. Not that he wanted anything to happen, but he was prepared—either way. Having all that inside information got his adrenalin pumping. He was in a whole new world—an exclusive club of information—and he loved it. As Henry daydreamed about what might be, he was suddenly interrupted.

"Mr. Larson, sir?"

Henry looked up at his driver. "What is it, Mo?"

"Sir, do you mind? I cannot work tomorrow. I know it's short notice, but I will need the day off, sir."

How unfortunate, Henry thought. He needed him tomorrow, if nothing else, as a witness. "Why tomorrow, Mo? Can't you do whatever you need to on Wednesday or Thursday? I need you tomorrow. I'm driving my daughter to school. What's so important that…" Henry caught himself in mid-sentence. Coincidence? Why was Mo (short for Muhammad) asking for the day off? Could he have heard rumors of the attack? Could that be possible? It was a pretty big coincidence, he thought.

"What's the emergency, Mo?"

Mo hesitated. "Uh, it's, it's uh, it's my wife. She's sick. She needs to go to doctor."

"Really? What's wrong with her?"

Again, Mo hesitated. Henry noticed Mo was fumbling his answers and felt that Mo was hiding something. Clearly there was something Mo was not telling Henry. Did he have information? Henry had gotten his information from the U.S. Military. Where would Mo get his from—the Muslims? Still, Henry pressed Mo.

"Mo, I need you tomorrow, so I'll hear no more about you needing the day off. Is that clear? You can take your wife to the doctor after you drop me off, can't you?"

Mo nodded as if to say "yes." He dropped Henry at home without another word being spoken.

That night Henry kept to himself, staring at, but not watching the T.V. Kate called him to bed around 11:00 pm, but he declined. He couldn't stop thinking about Samantha. What if something bad happened to her? Dare he call, even now, to warn her? These feelings were constantly overtaken by those of fear, fear that his relationship with her would be exposed, and fear that his reputation would be tarnished. Funny, he never considered that people already thought the worst of him. He finally dragged himself to bed at about 2:00 am. He tossed and turned all night, constantly checking the clock, waiting for the 6:00 am alarm. It seemed like forever. Whenever he fell asleep, he would awaken, hoping it was time, only to find that mere minutes had passed. When 6 am finally arrived, Henry had logged less than an hour of sleep, yet he was not tired. There was too much going on in that head of his. And his body was hours away from telling his brain just how tired it was. As Henry sprang from bed to shower, he no longer wondered if something was imminent that day. He was sure of it.

# CHAPTER 9

▼

# D-DAY

**Tuesday, September 11<sup>th</sup>, 2001, 6:00 am.**

Glen Larson also awoke to his alarm. He waited just a minute as he pondered his day. As he showered, he played in his mind all the possibilities of what might happen this day. Some scenarios have him and Henry laughing at the end of the day, wondering how gullible they were, and thinking they were actually privy to some deep government secret. Other scenarios are frightening, and Glen finds himself somewhat shaken by these thoughts. But even the very worst scenario his mind can think up won't approach what reality he would soon face. As he towel-dried himself, his only thought was to get to work and put an end to all of this. He dressed and headed downstairs to hail a cab. It's a beautiful sunny day, an unseasonably warm 75 degrees. As he waited for a cab, he observed the usual hustle of the morning rush. On the outside it looked like a normal day. It was hard to imagine anything bad could happen on such a magnificent day, he thought. Just then a cab pulled over and he was on his way downtown. As the car got within a few blocks of the Trade Center, his eyes fixated on the Towers. He can't help but stare at them the rest of the way. His cab pulled up in front of the trade center, and just like every other day, Glen slowly exited the cab. The car pulled away, leaving Glen standing alone in front of the north Tower. It was 7:30 am and curiously quiet outside the Trade Center on West Street. Glen couldn't put his finger on it, but something was different. It seemed more like a Saturday than a weekday. Then it hit him. Where was everyone? On a normal day there were thirty to forty cabs cluttered around the Trade Center looking for fares. But Glen noticed that today there were none. Waiting a few minutes, he observed an occasional cab drop-off. But instead of the cab staying around, waiting for a pick-up or going next door where the Marriott Hotel was, they simply sped away. It was eerie, he thought. It was well known that most city cab drivers were of Muslin descent. The fact that this particular morning they were curiously absent could not be a coincidence, Glen thought. All of a sudden he no longer felt like he was the only one who knew something. I mean on a daily basis, police would routinely have to chase dozens of the cluttered cabs away—but not today. Today there wasn't a one. This scared Glen a little. He found himself unable to take that next step into the Trade Center. His heart began to beat a little faster, but he knew he had to go in. He took a slow deep breath and exhaled. He then slowly walked into the North Tower of the World Trade Center. As he rode up in the elevator, he counted the floors to himself until it reached 99. He exited the elevator and began his final journey to his office. Passing the company receptionist, Judy, he smiled and gave a big "hello," the kind you remember. This morning he took the scenic route to his office, around several other trading desks where traders and brokers were in early. He made sure several of them saw him and stopped to say good morning to a few, just to be sure. As he arrived at his office, he spotted Tom Raferty and Louie Vitale, two co-workers who had arrived before him. He has known both Tom and Louie since he arrived at the firm, some eight years ago.

Tom Raferty, who was simply called "Raff," was a twenty-six year old of pure Irish decent. Tommy lived and worked for two things: sports and weekends. He had been somewhat of an accomplished tennis player, until elbow problems caused him to give it up at the age of 18. Before that he had been courted by several colleges and even finished third in the Junior Nationals. He was the guy who, by the end of a party, had rarely failed to do something that people would talk about the next day.

Now Louie Vitale, or "rude Lou" as he was known, was the exact opposite. Louie was a dapper-dressing Brooklyn Italian. He knew every mobster hangout and treated anyone he didn't know as if they had robbed his mother. Hence the name, "rude Lou," but once you got to know him he was a sincere, giving friend, one who would not turn his back on you. They were two unlikely friends, but inseparable, and two of Glen's closest buddies.

Almost every Thursday the three of them frequented the "Pipeline," a bar across West Street, overlooking the water. It was "the place" to go on Thursdays, as lots of young single women flocked there in search of a potential Wall Street suitor. Usually by the end of a typical night Glen would be the first to surrender, going home by midnight. Louie and Raff would virtually close the place and crawl home about 3:00 am. Most Fridays, Louie and Raff rarely made it in before 9:00.

This morning they were both agonizing over the Giants' Monday night loss to Denver.

"Did you see that disgrace last night, Glen?"

"Yeah, Raff, it's gonna be a long year."

Louie offered Glen a cup of coffee, but Glen simply shook his head, "No thanks, Louie. I'm okay."

"Not me," Louie complained. "I'll be pounding this shit all day to stay awake. You know, it's one thing to stay up on a Monday night if you win, but when you lose like that, there isn't enough coffee to justify it."

Glen couldn't take it anymore. For the first time he realized Henry's plan didn't account for looking friends in the eye and then leaving them in potentially life-threatening danger. This, without so much as a hint of a warning, seemed very cold to Glen. He actually had a few friends in the firm, unlike his brother.

"You're right, Louie; you're absolutely right."

After rustling around his desk for a few more minutes, Glen nervously looked at his watch. It was already 8:05 am and he was running behind his brother's imposed "be out by 7:45 am" schedule. Glen quickly headed for the exit, this time taking the shorter route to the elevators. He made his way down to the lobby. All the while he was in the elevator, Glen could hear his heart pounding with anticipation, each beat louder as he got closer to the lobby. When the elevator doors finally opened, he exited, with a sigh of relief. Glen hurried out the doors to West Street, once again noticing the absence of traffic in front of the Towers. Still, there were no cabs! This was absurd. 8 am and no cabs, he thought. He looked down toward the South Tower in front of the Marriott to see if there might be some there—nothing. He was getting anxious now, as it was several minutes after 8:00 am. He looked up to admire the towers one last time before hurrying back through the building toward the PATH Trains that would take him to New Jersey and his appointment with his brother. Although Henry had been very clear not to take the trains, Glen had no choice. Neither he nor Henry could have foreseen there being no taxis outside the busiest building in New York.

As his train arrived at the Newark terminal, Glen quickly made his way up the stairs to the main concourse. He walked into the terminal coffee shop and again looked at his watch: 8:35 am. He was late, but nothing had happened, so he calmly sat down and ordered a cup of coffee and a bagel while he opened up a newspaper. Now all he had to do was wait. He kept trying to reassure himself:

This is ridiculous, nothing is going to happen. He repeated this to himself over and over again. This thought helped calm him. What he didn't know was that by that time the fate of thousands of people was already in motion. While he was engaged in chat with his two friends, Louie and Raff, some thirty-five minutes earlier in three airports—Boston's Logan, Washington's Dulles and Newark's International—groups of terrorists were boarding airplanes. The first two planes to be hijacked had just left Boston. American Airlines flight number 11 departed at 8:00 am, bound for Los Angeles, and the other—United Airlines flight 175— left five minutes later, bound for San Francisco. Aboard these planes were trained cold-blooded killers, willing to perform an act like none before them. Their mission was so secret even they did not know who amongst them was involved. All they knew was that once their respective planes took off they would put on bandanas given to them weeks earlier. They would all be red except one. That one was green. He who wore the green bandana would symbolize the leader of the group and the one to fly the plane. At least two per plane were trained pilots whose job would be to dispose of the airplanes' pilots and take over flying the planes. To add insult to injury, they were trained by Americans on American soil in American schools. Once the planes took off, those with red bandanas would storm the cockpit, killing anyone in their way, whether they were pilots, flight attendants or passengers. They carried knives and box cutters to do their job. As most hijackings were designed in the past to steal a plane and take it to a safe destination, the hijackers felt sure they would meet with little resistance, and they were right. Once they had control of the cockpit, the leader would take control of flying the plane, while the others guarded the door from any would-be hero passengers. They would try to put passengers at ease by lying to them over the plane's intercom. They told passengers to "be calm"—that they just wanted to fly somewhere safe—and if the passengers remained calm in their seats, it would all be over soon. That part was true.

As the terrorists were making their way toward Manhattan, Henry was busy being a dad. When his driver, Mo, failed to show up as Henry had feared, he had no choice but to drive himself. Henry arrived at Courtney's school by 7:30 am and mingled with teachers and other parents until about 8:00 am. By then it was time for school to start, and all the parents were leaving. Henry headed for the Newark train terminal where Glen was waiting for him. He was moving slowly through traffic at 8:40 am while the first plane was screaming toward the North Tower, where his helpless employees were just starting their day, some busy with early trading, while most others were just having their morning coffee and bagel or reading the morning paper. They had no idea of the fate that was headed their way. They were just going about their daily routines. They hadn't done anything to provoke such an attack, but they were about to learn, yet again, how these cowards fight, preying on innocent unarmed men, women and children for no reason other than to create a state of fear.

At the same time, Jim Swimhammer and Rick Stein were driving uptown for their 9:00 am meeting. Just then a screeching, unforgettable shriek came over the downtown area. Tourists and residents looked up in horror as they witnessed the huge jetliner, American Airlines flight 11, above them, racing toward the Tower. Seconds later it struck. The first plane crashed smack into the middle of the North Tower, the tower occupied by Catalano Securities. It struck at almost the top, hitting at approximately the 90th floor. The force of the impact rocked the building back and forth as much as fifteen to twenty feet. Just seconds later the plane's fuselage ignited, causing a massive explosion. People, both in the plane and in the Trade Center, were incinerated immediately. Fires were raging at almost 2,000 degrees, some 800 degrees higher that that of someone being cremated! Floors of debris and bodies were sent skyward, cascading to the surrounding streets. Unlike what happened in '93, this time there was immediate chaos both inside and outside the buildings.

As Henry approached the Newark train terminal, he could see the black smoke pouring out of the tower across the river. There was nothing on the radio yet, as it was just minutes after the attack and no news agency had had time to report on it yet. A few minutes later, Henry parked his car quickly and scurried into the terminal. There, he found Glen, like several others, staring at the coffee shop TV in horror. By then it was all over the radio and TV. Glen spotted Henry and tried to speak.

"It was a plane, Henry! A fucking plane! I was there twenty minutes ago! Holy shit! Holy shit, Henry, what do we do?"

Henry tried to calm him, looking around, making sure no one was listening to them, but everyone's focus was on the little T.V. above the counter.

"Quiet, Glen. C'mon outside with me."

They walked outside towards Henry's car, but all the while they couldn't avoid staring right across the water at the burning North Tower.

"It's right by our office, Henry. People are dead. What the fuck did we do?"

"We? We…are you shitting me? We didn't do anything. We're not responsible for this, Glen."

"But we knew, Henry. We knew and we didn't do a fucking thing about it!"

"Calm down, Glen. We gotta think this thing through. We knew this was possible."

They both stared across the water, watching as the black smoke continued to pour out of the building. It was now 9:02 am.

"I didn't think a plane would hit us, Henry. Did you?"

Glen looked at Henry, but before he could answer a second explosion erupted. As they looked back, they could only see a cloud of fire and smoke coming from the other tower. A second plane, United Airlines flight 175, had struck the South Tower, this one with more precision than the first. The plane struck one side of the South Tower, almost knocking off the top of it. The force of the impact with the explosion and heat destroyed several important structural beams. This caused this Tower to eventually fall first, as the heat from the fires melted what few beams survived its initial blast.

"Oh, my God!" Glen shouted, while covering his mouth.

Now Henry, himself, was shaking, but still managed to stay in control. "Glen…Glen! Look at me. Here's what we're gonna do. You're going to call 911 and identify yourself right now! Remember the plan. Tell them you're stuck in the building and trying to get out…that you need help. Use your cell phone; tell them lines are out and the others are tied up. Talk fast and act scared. Then later on we'll say you made your way down a smoke-filled stairway with the other survivors. Through all this confusion, no one will ask any questions. Glen, are you listening to me?"

Glen was numb. All he could do was stare across the East River in shock at the site of both towers—once mighty but now looking frail—with smoke and flames pouring out. Glen remembered everyone he had talked to that morning: Judy the receptionist—shit, she was only 22, he thought. Then there were Louie Vitale and Tommy Raferty. How could he just leave them up there? They were his friends. He had thought about taking them with him, but he knew Henry would go ballistic, so he left them.

"Glen, are you with me?"

Somehow Glen gained enough composure to open his phone and dial 911. When the operator answered, Glen followed the script Henry had given him.

"This is Glen, Glen Larson. I'm in the North Tower. There's been an explosion. There's smoke…how do we get out? I'm trying…" he hung up in the middle of a sentence as if he were cut off.

"Perfect, Glen. Now turn off the phone."

"Why do I have to turn off my phone?"

"Because I don't want you answering it, even by accident. Leave it off until we figure this out."

Now everything was set, or so Henry thought.

"Where do I go now, Henry?"

Henry pondered for just a minute. "Just down the block is a Motel 6. Go there; check in under Glen Smith. Don't use a credit card; pay cash. I'll call you when it's the right time and come back to pick you up. Hopefully it should only be a few hours."

"What are you going to do, Henry?"

Henry looked up. "Me, I'm, uh, going to check on the company", and he pointed across the river at the burning North Tower. Henry got into his car and hurried toward Manhattan. While he was devising ways to deceive his employees, they were fighting for their very lives. When the first plane hit the North Tower, the explosion of jet fuel sent flames throughout the 90$^{th}$ to 99$^{th}$ floors. This of course, was right at the heart of Catalano Securities. The people were helpless, as the burning jet had destroyed all elevators and stairwells. Groups of employees tried everything possible. Gary Short led a group up to the roof, trying to find fresh air, only to encounter a locked door. They never got any further. Louie Vitale, Tom Raferty and several others gathered in a conference room on the opposite side of the building, where smoke had not made its way yet. That solution, however, was temporary. Soon the heat and smoke found them as well. They broke open some windows, but that only served to fuel the fire. Some decided to take matters into their own hands, refusing to fall victim to 2000-degree incineration. Those people made their final act a plunge from the 99 floors, where only traces of them would be left once the ground finished with them. Many made their last calls to loved ones before the second plane cut out the phones. Some told of heat so unbearable they could no longer stand on the floor. Computers were literally melting in front of them. They simply told family or friends they loved them, then surrendered to their destiny. Samantha O'Hara ran to Henry's office. Naturally, she found it empty. Still, she went in and sat at his desk. As the smoke thickened and heat became unbearable, she curled up in his chair, weeping for their unborn child. She stayed there until the Tower fell.

These were the images Henry would never see, or even imagine. His sick, twisted, selfish mind would not allow it. As was his lifelong trademark, he focused on how everything affected only him.

While driving through the Holland Tunnel, Henry was rehearsing a would-be speech. Even he had no idea what chaos he was about to observe. Once out of the tunnel, all traffic came to a stop. For fear of some other kind of attack, Mayor Giuliani had ordered all bridges and tunnels shut down immediately. This meant drivers had to leave their cars wherever they were and walk. Police were directing people away from the downtown area and the towers, but Henry walked right toward them. As he got within a few blocks, the sight of falling debris and bodies stunned him. He witnessed people jumping to certain death from the upper floors. Some were surely Catalano employees. For a split second a feeling of guilt came over him. He looked down at the ground, grimacing as he felt a sickness in his stomach. After a few moments, that passed and he continued moving toward the Towers. He got to the corner of West and Vesey Street, finding himself directly in front of the North Tower, before he was ushered away by police who were clearing the area. He didn't get very far before the ground began to rumble. Like an earthquake, the ground began shaking all around him. Henry asked people running from the buildings what floor and building they had come from, but there was too much chaos; people were screaming and running for safety. As Henry peered up, he saw the once mighty South Tower begin its collapse. Henry followed the crowd running up West Street before making his way into a bar with several other frightened victims. The South Tower was down within a matter of seconds, slicing through the Marriott Hotel on it's way down, some pieces landing clear across West Street and crashing into the atrium of the World Financial Center. Then came the cloud of dust and ash, racing through the streets as fiercely as a hurricane, carrying the remains of the South Tower and it's occupants. It was like a large dark cloud had landed in lower Manhattan. There were no words to describe the scene. As Henry looked around, all he saw was people staring in horror.

"What the hell is happening and when does it end?" he thought. Minutes later, Henry pulled himself together. He went outside, despite several other people's pleas that he stays. He had to get some information. Staying inside that bar watching the events like a deer in the headlight wasn't going to accomplish anything. He took out a handkerchief and put it over his mouth to protect his lungs from the scorching black smoke as he searched through the heavy fog-like dust until he found a working phone booth, then he called the hotel where Glen was waiting. When Glen picked up the phone, Henry delivered the bad news.

"Glen, you gotta wait there. I don't know how many of them got out!" The other end of the phone was silent. "Glen, are you there?"

"Yeah, I'm here, Henry. I'm watching this on TV. They just..." Henry stopped him in mid-sentence.

"Call you back, Glen."

Henry had spotted a news crew interviewing survivors on the street. He hung up the phone and quickly made his way toward them. He noticed all of them were covered in ashes, even the T.V. reporters. Here he was in a clean blue suit, with not so much as a smudge on it. Before he got to the cameras, Henry reached down, grabbing handfuls of ashes. Never considering what remains were in his hands, he quickly wiped them over his suit and on his face. Looking more like a victim, he moved up to where the interviews were being conducted. He listened carefully to see if anyone close to his floors were among those being interviewed. There were none. Then the reporter turned to him and started asking Henry if he was in the buildings. Henry paused a moment. He was not prepared to answer any questions, but quickly seized the moment. He couldn't resist.

"I'm trying to see if any of my people made it out. They're up on the 99th floor." He pointed to the remaining Tower standing. "They won't let me get any closer. My brother is up there. I have to find out!"

Then Henry buried his head in his handkerchief, protecting himself from the ash-filled cloud that was still upon them. Of course his true motive behind asking these questions was to find out if anyone from Catalano Securities had, in fact, survived. Glen was on record with 911, saying he was up there. If no one survived, then how would Glen have made it out? Surely someone would ask questions, and there were no answers. Henry feared this might lead to an investigation. How convenient that a select few board members—all of Henry's supporters—and Glen and Henry were not in the building. Maybe they would think it was a coincidence, but Henry's paranoia wasn't willing to take that chance, especially since he conveniently had been absent from the bombing in '93 as well. He strolled away from the reporter, leaving her with the illusion that he was emotionally unable to continue. He made his way into another bar several blocks from the Towers, where there were literally hundreds of people frantically watching the event on its TV.

At 10:29 am Henry witnessed the unimaginable. The North Tower buckled for just a second, and then crumbled like a house of cards. When it fell, Henry found himself dumbfounded. Even he hadn't considered something as hideous as this happening. As the rumbling stopped, once again the black clouds came. They covered lower Manhattan like a blanket. It looked like midnight or the end of the world, Henry thought. He knew he was fucked. His perfect plan had a flaw—a big one. No one would make it out from any of the floors above the 85th. Now he couldn't help but think how stupid it was having Glen call and identify himself to 911. Little did he know how much this would stand out. It seemed the 911 operators received over 500 calls from within the Towers that morning, and only three people identified themselves with full names, Glen being one of them. And only moments ago, Henry, on TV, blurted out that his brother was up there! Now he had a real problem. How could he explain his dead brother being held up in a cheesy hotel in New Jersey? He watched the television, hoping there would be some way a few people escaped his building. He actually was angered when the networks cut over to cover some of the events of other hijacked planes. One had just missed the White House, striking the Pentagon, but Henry could care less. He had to regroup, get his head together, to figure a way out of this mess. His thoughts weren't on the several hundred employees he'd just lost. He concerned himself with one problem: getting away without people finding out what he knew.

Henry opened his cell phone and tried to call Jim Swimhammer, but his phone still did not work. It continued flashing "no service." He waited his turn for the one working payphone in the bar. Jim was gridlocked like everyone else in midtown Manhattan, but at least his phone was working.

"Jim?"

"Where are you, Henry? Are you okay?"

"I'm by the ferry. I can't get out of the city."

"Henry, did anyone make it out?"

"I don't know, Jim. There's no information."

After a short pause Jim asked, "Did you try calling up there before it fell?"

Henry looked down at his cell phone, realizing for the first time that he never even once tried to call a single person up in his company, not even his own secretary or Samantha O'Hara.

"I couldn't get through," he lied. Then once again he quickly changed the subject. "Jim, we need to meet."

"Where, how? Nothing is moving, Henry!

"You have a car. Can't you find a way down here? The drive might be open; take that."

"Fuck you, Henry! Nothing is open, and besides, I have Rick with me, remember?"

Henry couldn't cope with this kind of a situation. In the past he would have either bought or muscled his way out of any problem—until now.

"Fine! Find a way to get to New Jersey and call me. We have a problem."

"We have a problem? We have a problem? Are you fucking serious? The whole city has a problem. Thousands of families—they have a problem! What problem do you have Henry? Can't get your morning croissant because the vendor is buried under a building?"

Henry could see that Jim was irrational. He felt guilty, but Henry had no time to care. He continued to insist that Jim meet him.

Jim, realizing Henry would continue to harass him, begrudgingly agreed and angrily hung up, cursing Henry as he did so.

It was several hours before the police reopened any transportation out of Manhattan. Tunnels and bridges remained off limits for fear of other attacks, but some railways were able to operate. Private boats were transporting people from the South Ferry area to Staten Island and New Jersey. Henry patiently waited his turn and made his way back to Glen. It took Henry almost four hours to get back to Glen's motel. He could have made the same trip in fifteen minutes before all this happened. As he arrived, he noticed that his cell phone was back in operation.

Henry reached the hotel just before 3:00 pm. By then Glen was sufficiently sedated. Henry observed over two-dozen empty beer cans in the room. "How are you feelin', Glen?"

"Like a dead man, Henry like a fucking dead man. What do we do now?"

"We wait for Jim to call. I have an idea, but I need Jim's help to make it work."

Henry and Glen nervously paced the motel's small twelve-by-twelve room. All the while, it's television remained on, replaying and reminding the brothers of the events, which had led them to where they were.

It was almost 5:00 pm when Jim Swimhammer finally called. "I'm in East Rutherford, Henry. Where are you?"

"We're at the Motel 6 by the Newark train station."

"We? Who's *we*?"

"Never mind, Jim, just get here as soon as you can. Oh, and bring some food. We're starving here."

Jim shook his head, wondering what the hell he had gotten himself into. Was it worth it anymore? At first working for Catalano had seemed like a great opportunity, but now Jim was feeling "used" like every other employee had. Still, after stopping at a local Burger King, he headed toward the Motel 6 where Henry and Glen were waiting. It only took Jim thirty minutes to arrive, but to Glen and Henry it seemed like hours.

They had been staring at the TV as it continuously recapped the gruesome events of the day. Just prior to Jim arriving at the hotel Henry's cell phone rang—again. Thinking it was Jim he angrily picked it up. "Where the hell are you?"

The quivering voice on the other end surely was not that of Jim Swimhammer. "I'm home. My God Henry, I thought you were dead!" It was his wife, Kate. "Are you safe? Where are you? Why didn't you call?" She was frantically rambling on while obviously sobbing. In all the confusion, Henry had forgotten to call his own wife to tell her he was okay.

"I'm okay, honey, but my cell phone wouldn't work in the city."

"Where are you now?" she asked.

"Well, I had to leave my car in the city. They stopped all traffic."

"I know. I saw that on the TV," Kate interrupted.

"I'm making my way through New Jersey, but it's a slow move." Henry was desperately trying to change the subject. "The company, it's...it's gone! You saw it, right?"

Once again Henry was relying on his ability to divert attention away from the conversation and into one, which would provide sympathy toward his plight, even to his own wife.

"Is Glen okay?" Kate asked, almost reluctantly.

This was the moment of truth for Henry. As he stared into Glen's eyes, he slowly gave his verdict. "I don't know. I've tried to find out, but no one knows." Henry felt compelled to lie, even to his wife. In Henry's twisted way of thinking, no one could be trusted until this was worked out. No one! "I don't know when I'll get home, but don't worry. I'm with Jim Swimhammer. He has his car and will take me home. Honey, I can't talk. I promise I'll see you soon. Love you."

"I love you too, Henry," but Henry had already hung up before he could hear Kate's words.

A few minutes later, when Jim finally arrived, he was surprised to see Glen. Henry brought him up to speed on their failed plan. Jim shook his head in disbelief.

Jim, Glen and Henry sat down to a delectable meal of lukewarm hamburgers, soggy fries and watered down cokes as they discussed their situation. Henry started by attacking Jim.

"Shit, Jim, nice job! Maybe an attack? The whole fucking building is gone and Glen was supposed to be in there! What the hell do we do now?" All the while, Henry glanced over at Glen.

By now Jim was in no mood for Henry. The whole trip over he had contemplated how he could get away from Henry for good. "Don't blame me, you sick fuck! If not for me, you'd be at the bottom of that pile of rubble with the rest of your employees, as you should be! It's not my fault your cleverly disguised plan to deceive the world had a kink in it."

Henry couldn't bring himself to say "thank you" to Jim, so again he changed the subject. "Well, what do we do now? No one survived...no one, which means..."

"I know what it means, Henry," Jim interrupted. "It means he (pointing at Glen) is a dead man."

Glen, who by now felt like a pawn in their chess game, sat down and opened another beer. Henry looked over at his brother and tried to reassure him everything would be all right. "Listen, little brother, sleep here tonight. Don't call anyone, including me. We'll try to figure this out by the morning. Maybe we'll catch a break and someone will have made it out. Let's just wait and see."

By then Glen was so drunk he would have agreed to anything. As Henry and Jim left, they were walking toward Jim's car when Henry stopped. "After you drop me off tonight, come back to my house tomorrow at 8:00 am. And you'd better have some ideas."

Jim acknowledged, adding, "Henry, are they all gone?" referring to Catalano employees.

"Shit, Jim, I don't know! This isn't what I expected. I...I...we have got to figure out what the hell to do." Then Henry got into Jim's car and didn't speak to Jim for the rest of the forty-minute trip to his house. He sat there, staring into space, contemplating his fate and his next move. Jim occasionally peered over, observing Henry in deep thought.

"What a psycho I've gotten involved with," Jim thought.

It was after 8:00 pm and Kate was nervously waiting for Henry. When he finally walked through the door, she ran to console him. She began to cry, while holding Henry close to her.

"It's okay...I'm all right."

But Kate continued to cry. After a minute or so she let go of Henry, looking at him.

"Oh my God, you're a mess!"

Kate, like others, was fooled by Henry's ghostly appearance, with dust and debris on his suit. She hugged him and gave him a kiss, but Henry was very rigid.

"Are you sure you're okay?" she asked, fully expecting Henry to dwell on the events that left him virtually without a company and perhaps his own brother. She was a bit surprised by his response.

"Those cops suck. Not only did they shut down the tunnel, which is where my car is, they treated me like I was some tourist or 'schmuck' just trying to gawk at the Towers. Don't they know who I am? They all suck." Henry took off his soiled suit jacket and headed for the bathroom. "I need a shower."

Kate watched as the bathroom door closed behind him. Maybe he was in shock, she thought. Why else would he only be concerned about the lack of respect he felt the police showed him? He had just lost over 500 employees: people, flesh and blood with families, and in the most horrifying way imaginable. He must be in shock. If not, she would have to conclude that her husband was a self-centered careless monster, with no regard for any human life. He had to be in shock, right? And what about his brother? He never said a word. Knowing how her husband was, Kate decided to leave him be. "In time he'll come to me," she thought, but Henry went right to bed, falling into a deep sleep.

## September 12th, 2001, 7:00 am.

Kate woke Henry, who curiously slept late. Henry never over-slept. He was up at 6:00 am like clockwork everyday.

"Henry, it's 7:00 am."

Henry looked up at the clock and dragged himself up. By the time Jim Swimhammer arrived at 8:00 am, Henry had already consumed a breakfast of eggs, toast and coffee. He said virtually nothing to Kate, except to insist that the children stay home from school. Several times Kate tried to engage him in conversation, but Henry refused.

"I can't, honey. I need time. There is so much to do and I don't know where to start."

So again, Kate let him be. It was a new day and Henry had had all night to recover from the events of September 11th. The morning paper was a grim reminder of all the disastrous events that had taken place the day before. Not only were the Towers destroyed, part of the Pentagon was destroyed by the plane that was targeted for the White House. It overshot its target, but still managed to kill over 200 people when it struck the west side of the historic structure. Heroic passengers who were able to force the plane down into a wooded area of Pennsylvania overtook another hijacked plane. Though all of them died, they undoubtedly saved the lives of its intended target, somewhere in Washington D.C., believed to be either the Capitol Building, or perhaps another shot at the White House. None of this really interested Henry this morning; he was focused on his own situation.

After a short cup of coffee, Henry and Jim were on their way back to Newark and the tiny motel where Glen was holed up. Henry didn't want to say anything in front of Kate, so he waited until he was in Jim's car before talking, but before he could hatch his plan, Jim hit him with a bombshell.

"I quit, Henry. I've had enough."

Henry was in shock, "Jim, you can't quit now and leave me in this mess alone. We're a team."

"Don't rah-rah me, Henry. I'm not one of your brokers. I know what you're about. You hired me for information, and you got it. You got my salary's worth and then some. You and Glen are alive, but it's not worth it for me anymore."

Henry scrambled. He had to change Jim's mind. He truly needed him. "Jim, you are a big part of our future now. You will have a much bigger role with me and that means a lot more compensation. Can't you see that?"

"So what now, Henry? Are you gonna offer me one of your worthless partnerships or make some other hollow promises? I'm not taking the bait. I'll drop you off at the hotel, and then I'm finished."

Henry knew he needed Jim more now than ever. He also realized he would have to do whatever it would take to keep him on board. So he did.

"A million dollar bonus!"

"Huh? What are you talking about, Henry?"

"I'm talking about one million dollars, Jim. You deserve it, and I need you."

Jim paused while he pondered Henry's offer. He wasn't sure what was up Henry's sleeve. Even at that price, would it be worth it to stay in this crazy situation? Jim couldn't sleep for most of the previous night. He had been feeling guilty. He got a call from his brother and they both cried on the phone. Jim didn't blame Henry, but he didn't want to go on the way it was. But then again, maybe this was the payoff for taking all of Henry's shit. The more Jim thought about it, the clearer answer came to him. This was his opportunity, and it might never come again. He stared at Henry, while shaking his head from side to side. He decided to accept Henry's offer. After all, he knew this would probably be the only time he would have Henry over a barrel like this.

"Okay, Henry, a million dollar bonus and a salary raise to $300,000 a year!"

Henry paused, but only for a second. "Done!"

This was still a good deal for Henry. He thought of how many brokers he paid three times that much that were not as valuable to him as Jim was. Besides, this wasn't really going to cost Henry so much as a dime.

You see, on the night of September 11th, while families were trying to cope with their losses and the rest of the country with the fear of where the next terrorist attack might be coming from, Henry was doing what he does best: planning. He sat silent in Jim's car all the way home, thinking and plotting his next moves. He prepared no differently from how he had done in the past. Indifferent to his losses, he focused on his gains. The more he dwelled on the events that had happened, the more he realized the good fortune that was coming his way. He was rid of all those brokers he couldn't do away with just a year ago, and this would be without any major repercussion from the customers. It was not Henry's fault this time. For a year, Henry had tried to figure out a way to have his "order-takers" either quit without going to a competitor, or to buy them out. The problem was that if he fired them or forced them to quit, he couldn't stop them from going to competitors. As for buying them out, that would have cost millions. Now he didn't have to worry about either choice. His only concern was making sure their clients didn't harbor too much anger or ill will towards him. To do this, Henry would have to excel in a most difficult role—one he had never been any good at—playing the "good guy." This was not something he was accustomed to, but with so much at stake, it was a challenge he felt more than up to. As for paying Jim, Henry was sitting on a fifty-million dollar bonus pool of money that was due to his brokers at the end of the month. Catalano's year-end was September 30th. Therefore, the company had accrued a large amount of bonus money that was payable October 1st to its employees, but now almost all of them were gone. He would use this money for his own benefit, he thought. He did this, never feeling even the slightest bit of concern for whose family—or families—might be affected. The money Henry promised Jim, along with his raise, would come from their money, not one penny of his own.

"So, Jim, now that you're still on board, we need to focus on…what do we do with Glen? The world thinks he's dead."

"Then he's gotta stay dead, Henry."

Henry stared angrily at Jim, but all the while he really knew what Jim was saying was true. He had come to the same conclusion the night before. But how would Glen react? What would be the plan? Actually, Jim had a great idea.

"Here is the way I see it, Henry. Glen goes away. He's single with no steady girlfriend or family other than you. We get him down to the Florida Keys for a few weeks. By then I'll get him a new passport and a new identity. He can go to the Caribbean for a few years, then we'll re-evaluate and go from there."

"How are you going to get him all that stuff, Jim?"

Jim looked at Henry with a tight lip. "You know better than to even ask that question, Henry."

Henry nodded in agreement. He didn't even want to know at that point.

"But what if someone sees him down there?"

"Who, Henry? With the exception of you, me, and three other people, everyone else who knows him is dead!"

Henry slowly broke into a smile, but he still had a few more questions. "How do we get him to Florida?"

"We can't fly and can't rent a car. That creates a paper trail."

"Okay, Henry, the only logical way he can go is AMTRAK. You don't need to show identification to buy a ticket. I'll go down with him, get him settled, then come back. Should take no more than a few days."

"So now we just have to get Glen to agree?" asked Henry.

"We? Henry, that's your job. I suggest you use the same method you used on me." Jim, of course, was referring to the million-dollar bonus Henry had just promised him. "You should also understand you're gonna have to stock him with a lot of cash. As I said, we can't have any paper trails, no credit cards. Understand Henry?"

"Oh, I understand. Now I gotta make Glen understand."

Henry and Jim put the final touches on their plan in the motel parking lot, and then went in to sell Glen on it. Glen was very fidgety, and paced the floor of the tiny motel room like an expectant father while Henry and Jim made their proposal. When it was Henry's turn to speak, he grabbed his brother by the shoulders and peered directly into Glen's eyes.

"Glen, there is no other way but this one where things will turn out good for you."

"How is that, Henry? What are you doing, getting me a bigger hotel room?" Glen was obviously sober now and back to his old sarcastic self.

"No, my brother; let me fill in some of the blanks Jim left out. First of all, once we get you set up on an island—whichever one that may be—we will open a bank account in your new name. I'll deposit two million dollars in an account. You'll rent a place right on the ocean where you'll be drinking margaritas and getting massages for the next year. You'll live like a king. I promise."

"Yeah, and then what, Henry? All of a sudden I'm alive? How are you going to explain that? What, like I have amnesia? Why can't we just say that 911 call was someone else posing as me?"

"Be realistic, Glen. You're burning up in a building. People are jumping out of windows, for God's sake! There is chaos everywhere! Who is going to believe someone took the time to make believe they were you? No one, that's who! Besides, they could easily track the call to your cell phone. This is the only way. Glen, I'm your brother. I brought you into this. You have to trust me. I'll take care of this like I always do. Haven't I always been there for you?"

Glen nodded as if to say "yes."

"Then let me handle this. I promise I'll make it right. When I am done and this is over, you'll be very a wealthy man."

"How wealthy, Henry? If I've got to disappear and change my whole identity, I wanna know how wealthy, and I don't mean two million dollars."

Henry paused, glancing over at Jim, and then asked Jim to leave him alone with his brother. When Jim left, Henry went over and whispered into Glen's ear, ""Ten million, tax free. More than you ever wanted or could have dreamed."

Glen broke out laughing.

"What's funny about ten million dollars, Glen?"

"It's not about that, Henry. I just didn't think I'd see the day that you, my own brother, would pitch me like I was one of those suckers you sold your partnerships to."

"Glen, you're wrong."

"Stop! Henry, let's just finish what you started. Remember, I know the value of what Rapid Trading has with the brokers gone. And for me it's not ten million; it's twenty-five million!"

Now it was Henry's turn to laugh, but in doing so he put his arm around Glen's shoulders and gave him a hug. "I see I've taught you well, little brother."

They both smiled, and just as Henry was about to open the motel door to let Jim in on the good news, Glen stopped him. "Just one second. When do I get it, Henry? Not that I don't trust you."

"We'll set you up right away with what you'll need, and within six months the rest will make its way into your account. But even Jim cannot know about it, Glen. Deal?"

Glen nodded and opened the door. Jim walked in and saw both Glen and Henry smiling. "Good to see how well you two are taking this tragic event."

"Relax, Jim. I just ironed out the details with Glen. We're going with your plan. When do you want to start?"

Jim looked at Glen. "We've already started. You can't go back to get anything, so let's go. Henry, I can't be seen with you and Glen in the car so, you're on your own."

"That's not a problem, Jim. As a matter of fact, I have no more problems. Besides, while you're heading to Florida I'll be busy here. I have to mourn the death of a company. Call me when you've arrived in the Keys, but from this moment, never—and I mean never—use Glen's name in a cell phone conversation with me again."

Henry hugged Glen one more time. "Remember, Glen, you can't call anyone, especially me. I'll get in contact with you through Jim in a few days and we'll start everything in motion." After Glen and Jim left the motel room, Henry spotted Glen's cell phone on the dresser. He walked over, picked it up stared at it.

"You were my one mistake," he said out loud. Then he took the cell phone, smashed it onto the ground, after which he picked up the pieces and deposited them in a trashcan outside the motel room. He looked up as Jim and Glen pulled out of the parking lot. Glen gave Henry a wave as they passed by. Henry smiled, hoping to make Glen feel secure, then Henry starting thinking. He was fairly sure

Glen would be just fine, living the good life on the beach. Then he thought about what he had said to Jim Swimhammer.

He couldn't help but think about how true the statement he had just made was. All of his problems had disappeared. Once again, he thought of Samantha O'Hara. He wondered if she had come looking for him when the plane hit or when it became apparent she wouldn't survive. He felt sick, but he knew there was no other way. He looked across the river at the still smoldering hole that used to be the World Trade Center. He blew a kiss to Samantha. His eyes welled. Then he calmly went back to the Motel 6 that had been home to Glen and paid the bill in cash. He had the desk clerk call him a cab and he headed home. Henry now had to embark on the biggest public relations sell of his illustrious career.

He began by hiring the services of a top public relations firm. He wanted to leave no stone unturned in succeeding to sell his customers, the families of his former employees and the public of his sincerity and tragic loss. "How better to gain sympathy?" he thought.

The Travers Group was considered a top-rated public relations firm. Their history included three ex-presidents and several current senators. Henry felt this was the perfect firm for him to hire. He met with the firm's top man, Tom O'Brien, for several hours. O'Brien outlined what he felt Henry needed do so as not to come off as the greedy self-centered pig that he was. Of course O'Brien didn't know this. In fact, he had never heard of Henry Larson until he walked into his office that day. Henry simply told him he didn't want to appear insincere, since it was such a sensitive time. O'Brien schooled Henry well and even set up his first press conference. It was to be one of several in a forty-eight hour span, as Henry was his own commercial for self-pity. Unfortunately, O'Brien couldn't keep Henry from being himself away from the media. Just prior to his first television appearance, Henry ordered that all employees listed in the building on September 11th be declared no longer employed and ceased any further benefits or pay to their families. A colder or crueler act could not have been imagined.

As Henry addressed the media and fielded questions, several times he looked down and took long pauses. This gave viewers the illusion that he was losing his composure and was overwhelmed with grief by the tragedy. It was just that: an illusion. O'Brien was a master at manipulating the media, and he schooled Henry perfectly. It worked like a charm. Henry, during one of his interviews, sealed Glen's fate.

"I know how every family out there must feel. I, too, lost a member of my family: my brother Glen. But let me tell you this—every person up there was part of the Catalano family. A family that I was the father to..." Henry paused again, looked down, and then departed. It was an Oscar-winning performance that fooled everyone except those who truly knew him, but it accomplished what it needed to. He was extremely satisfied with himself and felt assured of the country's sympathy toward him. The world now could not possibly suspect that Henry had had any prior knowledge of what happened, he thought. There were other firms who lost large portions of their companies. Sandler O'Neal, a government trading firm from the top floor of the South Tower, lost more than half its people. Cantor Fitzgerald, who also occupied the North Tower and was one of the largest bond brokerage houses worldwide, lost seventy-five percent of it's one thousand employees. Marsh McLennan, an insurance company, was decimated as well. One firm on the 103$^{rd}$ floor of Tower II lost everyone. But it was Henry who would capitalize on all of it. Every network and talk show wanted Henry on their shows. He was quite a showman. He learned the trait quickly, and the media ate it up. His was the perfect tragedy for them to use as their example. Most other firms' leaders went down with the ship, so to speak, but Henry was spared, but why?

Henry's response was, "So I can help and be the one to make sure these families never want for anything."

Each time Henry exited his interviews; he couldn't help but think, I should have given O'Brien a bonus. This, for the perfect way he had prepared him.

Over the next few days Henry set up a meeting place for all the families of his former employees to get updates. He secured 100 rooms in the Marriot Hotel by LaGuardia airport and booked one of its conference rooms where families could meet and get updates. Once Jim Swimhammer got back from safely tucking Glen away in Florida, Henry put him in charge of acting as a liaison to the families. Meanwhile, Henry breezed through interview after interview. Each time, his performance got better, but never did he deviate from the script. However, on one occasion a young upstart CNN reporter who had taken the time to do her homework caught him off guard. "Mr. Larson, isn't it true that as you sit here somberly begging for firms to sympathize with you that you in fact stopped paying your employees?"

Henry was stunned, but only for a moment. Like a prizefighter that was caught with a lucky jab, he came roaring back. "They're gone. I have to accept that. We all do, but I still have a responsibility to those who represent Catalano." Henry referred to his overseas employees and the Rapid Trading group that were not in the Towers but in a remote location in Brooklyn. Henry had moved Rapid Trading a year prior to September because of all the contempt the rest of the firm had for them. They were perceived as traitors, as they represented the vehicle that might one day make Catalano employees obsolete.

"I will take care of them. Please, you may be assured of that."

Henry, on key, then buried his head in his hands, but to his surprise, there was another punch coming.

"Isn't it true that you are in possession of a rather large compensation pool of money, due to these people?"

Henry did his best to hide his anger. He wondered where the hell she was getting her information. Thank God she didn't know the amount of money in the pool.

"Well," he started slowly, "we do have that, but it's not been a good year. I wish it had been. Besides, that money is owed to certain people. We have to ascertain that, and then of course we will pay it out. But...but..." once again a pause, "all our records are lost. It will take some time to figure it out..." another short pause, this time reaching for his eyes as if to wipe away tears, "but, as God is my judge, we'll do it."

Henry tucked his head down into his lap. It almost looked as if he was taking a bow for yet his best performance. He left, as if he couldn't continue, but truly he was afraid a tougher question might be coming. Like a great actor, he left them standing. This was one person Henry would never let interview him again. However, the damage was done, and now family members started to speak out against him. All his good publicity, all those magnificent interviews, and one damn reporter was ruining it all. How did she know about the bonus pool? Obviously from a family member or ex-employee. Either way, it created some new waves for Henry. It was unfortunate, too, as he never intended to divulge the bonus pool to anyone except those left to collect it. As it turned out, it was just another bump in the road for Henry Larson. He soon found a way to use that money to not only satisfy his doubters, but as a device for long-term positive publicity.

By now Glen was lying on a white sandy beach in Key West under the name Brian Stevens. Jim had rented a small house for him on the outskirts of the Keys in a town called Marathon. It was quiet and consisted mostly of short-time renters—no one who would stick around long enough to even remember what Glen looked like. It was perfect for Glen. The house was only twenty or thirty steps away from the water. Every morning Glen would get up, walk out the back and take a swim. Once Jim felt Glen was settled, he headed back to New York. When Jim arrived back in New York, he wasted no time lashing out details of how he and Henry would have to proceed with Glen, but Henry had a much larger agenda for Jim. Besides handling the public relations job with the employees' families, Jim was Henry's new "boy." As Henry promised, Jim was now part of the inner circle of Catalano Securities. Henry had him elected to the Board of Directors as its new Secretary, replacing the deceased Gary Short. Jim became Henry's right-hand man overnight. Henry was now ready to convene the Board of Catalano & Feinberg for the first time since the September 11th tragedy. This was a short list, consisting of Len Abraham, Rick Stein, Jim Swimhammer and Henry. At this meeting, it was Henry's job to put together a plan, one that would not only put his former employees' families at ease but would keep the current ones from defecting—all this while eventually firing up Rapid Trading revenues. For the first time, he wouldn't have to deal with brokers whining to their customers. All Henry had to do was convince the clients that not doing business would hurt the families of those lost that fateful morning of September 11th. He had the upper hand at last with the very clients who had cut him down just one year ago by backing the brokers and refusing to do business. Henry had them in a position where if they didn't do business with the Rapid Trading system they would jeopardize any future earnings for the remaining families. This delighted Henry and he couldn't wait to present his plan to the board.

It was September 18th at 9:00 am, exactly one week after the attack on the World Trade Center and America. Despite futile search efforts by thousands of fire fighters and police from all over the country, no survivors from within the buildings had been found. The search had now become a recovery mission. How many bodies could they recover for the families? Each body found was taken from the site and draped in an American flag. Thousands of body parts were found and sent for DNA testing, in the hopes that a positive identification could bring some closure to the families of this horrible attack.

In Hoboken, New Jersey, the temporary home of Catalano Securities and Rapid Trading, Henry presided over his first official board meeting since 9-11. It was considerably lighter, as the only remaining members present were Rick Stein, Jim Swimhammer and Henry. The other surviving member, Len Abraham, was still in Tokyo, with no way to come to the meeting as airports were still closed down. He was present via telephone on conference speaker. So with everyone accounted for, Henry began the meeting. He started by saying how saddened he was on 9-11 and reminded them of his own loss: his brother Glen. He was grateful that by the grace of God those in attendance, for some reason, were spared this horrible fate. Now, with all the pleasantries aside, Henry was ready to get down to business.

"We have to go on, gentlemen. Our firms have to go on! But we must not forget about the families of those who perished last week. This is what we must do for the benefit of all. First, we will distribute twenty million dollars of bonus money. Rick and Len, I'm putting you two in charge of this. You're the only ones who knew what we could or should pay the brokers. You have thirty days to coordinate a list of where this money is to be paid."

Len interrupted Henry, "Henry, my people alone over here are owed over ten million. There has to be a lot more owed in New York. Where is the rest of the money?"

Henry snapped back angrily at Len. It seems Henry simply wanted his orders carried out without question. He didn't care how or what Rick and Len had to do to accomplish it.

"Listen up, all of you. We are going to have to provide for several hundred families going forward, so let me outline my plan and just carry it out! We have fifty million. Twenty million will be distributed in early November. I want your lists by mid-October. Then we will go to partners with an offer: their proposed bonus will include $100,000. For this they must relinquish all future claims toward Catalano and turn over their shares in the firm."

"Why would they do that?" Rick Stein chimed in.

Henry, once again angered, quickly turned toward Stein and responded, "Because, Rick, it will have been two months since they have received a pay check. Because, Rick, they'll want closure. Because, Rick, we'll remind them that with 90% of the employees gone, how could they expect to collect any future money from the partnership? And, last but not least, it will be just before the holidays. They'll want—no—they'll need the money. That's why, Rick. Now, may I continue?" Henry paused and then peered around the room. There were no more interruptions.

"Next, we'll agree to give 50% of all profits for the next seven years to the families. In addition, we'll agree to cover all the families medical benefits for this period as well." In his mind, Henry had it all figured out. He would take what was left of the bonus pool—thirty million—and hold it for the firm. He would use it to fund the medical coverage for the families, and Catalano would be able to post the profits for the next several quarters, using this money. He explained to the board how this would give the families the illusion that he was coming to their aid. It would also provide an answer to any pain-in-the-ass reporters questions as to how he was "helping" the families.

The board members were stunned. From a business prospective it was flawless. Still, it bothered them because the families were truly getting fucked. Len Abraham may have recapped it the best.

"So, as I understand it, Henry, we start by convincing the surviving employees to take less for the good of the deceased. We strong-arm the families to relinquish their partnerships for less than half of what their bonus should have been, but we give them this plan where we pay their insurance out of *their own* money and a percentage of the profits created by what's left of *their* bonus pool. Is that it in a nutshell, Henry?"

"I could not have said it better, Len. You have obviously grasped the concept."

Jim Swimhammer, who had been silent until then, spoke up. "I have a question. What happens to the plan if the money runs out before seven years?"

"Good question, Jim; nothing happens. The plan will say the families get the percentage of profits for seven years. Within two years there will be no profits. By then everything should be transferred into Rapid Trading, which we will make clear is not tied to Catalano Securities. I know what you're thinking, Jim. What do the clients do when this happens? I'll answer that, too. Also, nothing! By that time some won't even be trading, and others will have become comfortable doing business with Rapid. And remember, Jim, we were the good-guys all that time."

Len wasn't entirely thrilled with this plan. He was concerned as to how he would be able to control the surviving branch of Catalano, his group overseas. "If we screw these guys on their bonuses, what keeps them from leaving and going to our competitors?"

"Simple, Len; first of all they have contracts. They know how we are about that. Second, they would look like money-grubbing pigs, leaving their deceased partners' families to suffer. And last but not least, we would sue any firm dumb enough to hire them, not to mention make them look like monsters in all the papers. How could they have such little respect for the families who lost their spouses, moms, or dads in the Trade Center by taking food from their children's mouths?"

Len Abraham, Rick Stein and Jim Swimhammer were all disgusted and amazed how Henry, in only one week's time, could be so thorough as to dot every seeming "i" and cross every "t". He set up a plan so perfect, where everyone would get fucked except him. It was unbelievable. What none of these men realized was that once Henry succeeded in this part of his plan, they would be next.

CHAPTER 10

▼

# U.S. AND HENRY
# ATTACK

While the United States government was rounding up terrorists all over the world, it also launched a military strike at terrorism. The president had assured the country and the world of his resolve to bring Osama Bin Laden to justice. At the same time, Henry Larson launched his own attack; one that he hoped would net him the financial brass ring.

First on his list was his exiled brother, who by now was living like a king, as promised. After spending less than a month in the Florida Keys, Henry—with the help of Jim Swimhammer—was able to move Glen to a rented house in Bermuda. It was a beautiful three-bedroom, two thousand square foot cottage overlooking the ocean. It sat on a cliff two hundred feet high, with a view most people only dream about having. It was a two hundred, eighty-four step walk down a winding hill to pink sandy beaches and glorious ice-blue water. Henry had kept his word, and Glen—or Brian Stevens as he was now known—was sitting with over two million dollars in an overseas bank account. As planned, Henry's only contact with Glen was through Jim Swimhammer. When Glen needed to get a message to Henry, he called Jim's office, leaving his new name. Jim always called him back, but never from a cell phone. Henry arranged to meet Glen in the middle of October, when he took a much-needed vacation in Fort Lauderdale, Florida with his family. While Kate, Henry Jr. and Courtney played on the white, sandy beaches and bathed in the warm ocean waters, Henry was secretly off to see his brother. Glen took a boat from Bermuda to Miami, and then took a cab to Fort Lauderdale to meet Henry. There the two brothers met aboard a local gambling boat. Of course no one, not even Kate, knew this was the motive behind the vacation. Things were simmering down, and Henry's on-air performances were pretty much done. At first Henry didn't even recognize Glen. The last time he'd seen Glen was on September 12th, and he had dark black hair, brown eyes and glasses. Now, with the help of Jim Swimhammer, Brian Stevens wore no glasses and had blue eyes, courtesy of special contact lenses. He also had bleached blonde hair. Jim had done a wonderful job of transforming Glen. It was as if he was truly a different person. In fact, Henry didn't recognize him at first. It was Glen who spotted Henry and embraced his brother.

"Jesus, Glen, you look great! I guess this life agrees with you."

"It's great, Henry. The house is beautiful. It's on a two hundred foot cliff right on the ocean, and it's true—blondes do have more fun."

They both laughed. Over the next few hours the brothers enjoyed several drinks, while Henry filled Glen in on how well his plan was moving along.

"When I get back we'll begin buying out the partners."

"Why do you need to do that, Henry? I mean, eventually their partnerships won't be worth anything anyway, right?"

Henry smiled. "Remember '93, Glen?" Henry was referring, of course, to the previous attack on the towers.

"Of course. What's that got to do with anything?"

"Remember the policy—the one Jim pushed on me? The one I didn't want to buy?"

It took a second before Glen realized what Henry was talking about. Glen almost leaped out of his chair. "The fucking policy. Holy shit, I forgot!"

Henry was referring to the "Interruption of Business" insurance policy Jim Swimhammer convinced him to buy when he first came to the company. Henry knew that if he cashed in the policy all of the partners would be entitled to a portion of the money, almost one billion dollars! This was an amount Henry wasn't willing to share with anyone.

"What happens if they find out about it later on?"

"Not to worry, Glen. I have that covered. You see, once all the partners sign over their shares, they'll have no recourse. I'm making sure the document they sign covers that. No matter what transpires after they sign, they're out! They have an opportunity to find it now. If they do, good luck to them. Only three people know about it; you, Jim, and me. That's why I know they'll never find it."

"What about the insurance company? They'll know."

"Do you think they are going to come forward and say 'Hey, here's your billion dollars'? No way. They're waiting and hoping I never make the call. I mean, they gotta know it's coming, but they're in no rush to bring it up."

Henry had a few more drinks with Glen before the ship arrived back in Florida.

"Do you ever miss her, Henry?" Glen was referring, of course, to Samantha O'Hara, Henry's now-deceased girlfriend. Henry paused to reflect before answering. Until then he hadn't even realized that Glen knew about Samantha.

"Miss who, Glen...she who?"

Glen smiled at his brother. "Henry, c'mon...I'm your brother. Do you think I'm stupid?"

Henry realized there was no reason to lie to his brother. Samantha was dead and Glen was in exile. He smiled back at his brother before answering.

"Sometimes I do, Glen, but I guess it's all for the best. Besides, this was the only way she was going to let me out." Once again Henry paused. He thought about all the wonderful trips to London and Tokyo, the intimate moments Samantha and he had shared, but it was that last conversation they had that stood out most in his mind. The one they had September 10th. The one in which Henry knew everything in his life might change. The one that scared him and convinced him not telling her was for the best, for him, that is.

"Yeah, Glen, I do think of her."

They embraced one more time and agreed they would try to meet in about a month. "I'll tell Jim to let you know when, Glen. You take care." Henry was relieved that Glen was so happy. It was one less potential problem to worry about. Henry returned to meet Kate and the kids for dinner that night. Kate suggested they go to Benihana, a Japanese steakhouse. The kids liked the show they put on while cooking the food on a grill at the table. Tossing knives, flipping shrimp and igniting flames kept the kids both amused and quiet. It was a perfect time for her and Henry to talk, but Henry had little to say about his day other than he had had a business meeting. By now Kate was deep in denial as to Henry's demeanor. First she used September 11th as the excuse for his shutting her out. Since then she'd figured it was due to the loss of his brother, Glen. She felt sooner or later he would let her back into his life. The truth is she was too scared to think otherwise. As for little Henry and Courtney, they were bubbling with excitement as they told their dad of their exciting day at the beach, building mud castles, running in the water, they had a great day to talk to their dad about.

Henry smiled, but didn't hear a word they said. His mind was elsewhere. He was obsessing on how to get back the partners' shares in the company.

The next day Henry took his family back home to New York. It was time to begin his quest. He needed to get back all the shares in Catalano Securities. On the trip home, Henry thought about his brother. Not the way you might think, however. He methodically made sure he did nothing illegal—nothing that could come back to haunt him, should Glen be discovered. Although Glen had a hefty life insurance policy, Henry never attempted to collect on it. That would be fraud, a very jailable offense. Hell, he didn't even have a memorial for him. If Henry should somehow be found out, surely he would face the wrath of Wall Street and most certainly the public, because of all his interviews designed to gain him sympathy. But Henry did nothing illegal, nothing that could cause him to be arrested, or worse jeopardize his license to do business. He felt this part of his plan was secure. On the plane trip home, Henry wondered if he should tell Kate. She was very distraught over Glen's apparent death, and there were times Henry almost told her. Still, what if she were to even accidentally mention it where someone else could overhear them. As much as he wanted to tell his wife, once again he let his fears dictate otherwise. She, like everyone else, would have to be kept in the dark.

When October 17th arrived, it was time for Len Abraham and Rick Stein to submit all employee bonus numbers. This included those employees who had vanished only one short month before. It was the first time Len had come to the New York area since the attack on the Towers. He was left speechless at what he saw. He was allowed a close look at the sight from an observation deck built for family members of those lost that day. He couldn't believe the sight of twisted rubble and smoke and ash that was once the Twin Towers. Television did the tragedy no justice, he thought. Being there was a taste of reality. He had been in that office a thousand times, and as he stood staring, his eyes welled as he thought of friends and co-workers gone forever. He stayed, staring at the sight, for nearly 30 minutes before somberly heading back to Catalano's temporary offices for his meeting with Rick Stein and Henry. The three men met in Henry's office and hashed out numbers for several hours. Len was getting strong resistance from some of his people. Seemed some of them weren't as stupid as Henry thought. A group of them threatened to leave, claiming breech of contract, and Len wanted to make sure Henry understood this before they finalized their numbers.

"Henry, these guys talked to a lawyer and they're gonna go if we don't pay what we owe them."

Unfazed, Henry stuck to his guns. "We have a plan, Len, and we're sticking with it. They have contracts; we'll sue them. They know this, right?"

"Yeah, Henry, they know. They also know that their contracts call for them to receive a 40% payout and the bonus we're paying them reflects a 20% payout. That's breech of contract on us!"

The "payout" referred to how brokers were compensated for their business. For example, if a client did $100,000 dollars worth of business, the company would get $60,000, while the brokers would get $40,000.

"Well, I'll tell you this, Len. Wherever they go, that firm is fucked! I will use every contact I have to do so. The press will have a field day with this, and I'll make sure they get our version of the story first. Don't they realize how the media loves me? I'm the good guy, and they're gonna look bad on this one."

"So we just let them go, Henry? That's it?"

"No, Len, that's not it. Since you're sure they're leaving, cut them back 10% more on their bonuses and use the money to keep some others from trying the same."

Len could only shake his head in disbelief. He couldn't understand why Henry was willing to let a profitable group walk out the door.

"So we just let millions go out the door? You know others will follow!"

"No they won't, Len, because the day—and I mean the day—those guys walk, we're gonna serve them and the company they go to with legal papers. Every employee left will pick up the paper and know that it will cost them a hundred thousand or more in legal fees to try to leave us. Every firm considering hiring them will know the same. We'll see who has the stomach for it. They know I do! Do you, Len?"

Len nodded "yes," but still questioned Henry as to his logic on this matter.

"Len, shut-up, listen and learn. We are gonna make these guys look so bad...you can't imagine. We're talking front page! Before they get to say a word to their customers, the world will think they're greedy bastards! Trust me on this, Len. It's been well thought out."

Len wasn't happy, but what could he do? He knew Henry had made up his mind, and that meant no matter how long he tried, he was not going to change it. He shut his mouth, and the meeting moved on. As it turned out, Len Abraham proved to be correct. Less than a week later, seven Catalano employees quit the firm to go work for competitors. They had every legal right to do so, as Len explained Catalano had under-paid them by 20%, as prescribed in their contracts. Although they were very aware of Henry's threat, they refused to be used by Henry. They knew he was using the victims and their families as an excuse to fuck them, and ultimately they felt they had to leave. Henry, too, kept his word. The day those brokers quit, they were served a lawsuit for "breach of contract" by Catalano Securities.. Their new employer, Fundamental Brokers, was also served, claiming they had interfered with their business by stealing employees under contract. The next morning both the Daily News and New York Newsday carried the story on the front page. Catalano supplied pictures of the employees for the tabloids, who boldly put "Traitors" over them as a headline. Henry knew what he was talking about. No one really even cared to hear his or her side of the story. Henry, once again, got more publicity. Henry wanted all of Wall Street, and America, on his side. For the most part, he got it. By the time those suits were settled it was page twelve news, not page one. The story was basically buried. By then no one cared; it was yesterday's news. Besides, Henry got another six months of free positive publicity. What Len and Rick Stein didn't understand was that Henry didn't care if his overseas desk quit. After all, those were partners he needed to rid himself of. By getting them to quit, they forfeited their partnerships, and as a bonus Henry could sue them and their new employers. The worst that would happen is he might lose, as he did, but he still got the insurance money and wouldn't have to buy out their partnerships. Besides, these guys didn't do any business for Rapid Trading, so why should he care?

As the meeting came to an end, Henry took a list of all those who perished on September 11th and divided it into three sections. The plan was to "divide and conquer." Henry got the top third percent of highest earners, consisting of mostly former desk heads and all officers of the firm. Len and Rick took the other two thirds, divided into middle-tier brokers and support personal. Henry felt these would be the easier of the groups, as none of the support help were even partners. They would be glad to get whatever the firm offered, nothing else. The middle-tier brokers were the families suffering the most. Even though these guys made between two and four-hundred thousand dollars a year, most of them lived way above their means, never realizing some day the gravy-train would come to a screeching halt. Henry figured that by November, most of these families would be so financially strapped they would jump at the offer about to be presented to them. Now Henry, he had the tough group. These were guys making anywhere from seven hundred and fifty thousand dollars a year well into the millions. Some of these widows might be a little headstrong or bring in lawyers or who knows what. That's why Henry took this group. It was the group that presented a challenge for him. Of course he never doubted his ability to succeed. Before the meeting broke up, Henry set a timetable for completing the job set forth. He figured it would take no more than a week to have the lower group finished and signed up.

The middle tier may present a couple of problems, but should take certainly no more than three weeks to finish. Of course, as for his group, Henry confidently boasted that he would probably be finished before Len and Rick. They agreed to meet on every Monday. At each meeting they would recap what percentage of the families had signed and let Henry know if any were going to be a problem. Henry instructed Len and Rick to follow the same guidelines while speaking with the families and/or their lawyers.

"Make sure these people realize that unless they all agree, no one gets paid. Remind them that others are sacrificing for them and that 50% of future profits will go to them, not to mention free medical coverage for their families. To close the deal, make sure they understand that they have a right to seek claims from the Red Cross and United Way in addition to what we give them and, that down the road they will get a big payout from the government in the form of a settlement. That should be enough ammunition to close the deals."

Just then Rick Stein, who hadn't said much to that point, mumbled something under his breath.

"What, Rick? What is it?"

"Nothing Henry. I couldn't help but think how fucking cold this is. Some of these people haven't even come to grips with this yet. Shit, they're not even all buried or had memorials. This is fucking sadistic and God damned cruel. Do you give a shit about anyone anymore but yourself?"

"How can you say that, Rick? I mean, you're still here, aren't you?" Would you prefer not to be?"

"Don't pull that shit on me, Henry. If I go, you don't have enough to represent a board, and that means nothing passes—no decisions. You could lose your authority."

Henry slammed his hand down, making a thunderous sound.

"You ungrateful prick! I saved your fucking life and this is your gratitude? I didn't see you coming up with any great ideas."

"Saved my life? What the fuck are you talking about?"

Henry looked over and saw Jim Swimhammer glaring at him. Jim didn't say a word, but his look sent Henry the message. Henry, of course, was referring to sending Rick uptown on the morning of September 11th, but he knew he couldn't tell him that. He recovered as best he could without revealing his true feelings.

"I gave you this board position. I took you from being an everyday broker to making millions as a member of this board. Besides, these people will be fine between the government and the charities. They'll get by just fine. So grow a pair of balls and do your job. And incidentally, I'll have a new board member in here five minutes before I accept your resignation. Don't for one second think you're smarter than me!"

This, of course, was a huge bluff on Henry's part. If Rick resigned, the partners could hold up any future decisions for months, but Henry's will was one that made every bluff seem real. Rick nodded his head in compliance and sat back down like a beaten puppy.

Henry continued, while walking around the conference room table where each board member was seated. He stopped and put his hand on Rick Stein's shoulder, as a father would who had just scolded his son.

"Now I know this whole thing has put stress on a lot of us, but we need to pull together. All of us need to go forward." This was Henry's own version of "good-cop, bad-cop." Normally you need two people to play that game. Obviously growing up Henry had so few friends he had learned to play the game by himself.

# CHAPTER 11

▼

# MOVING ON

There were several hundred funerals and memorials representing the families of Catalano Securities. Clearly Henry couldn't possibly attend them all, nor did he really want to. He did make sure to attend all memorials for his top employees and desk managers. He would often make only a brief appearance, but he made sure he was seen, usually arriving just minutes before the actual memorial began and walking up and down church aisles as if he were looking for someone. This enabled him to be sure that someone from the deceased family knew he was in attendance. This was just another one of Tom O'Brien's little tricks, and a very effective one. Shortly thereafter, Henry figured that his mere attendance at a loved one's funeral was enough to keep him in these families' good graces. This, he felt, would help him in his quest to acquire their partnership shares. Now, when he would call one of them up, they would gladly take his call. Whereas Len and Rick had to physically go to hundreds of homes of the deceased, Henry couldn't be bothered making all those trips. His plan was to call them up, make an emotional plea, and within an hour have a lawyer knocking on their door with an agreement. The mere thought of such an act by anyone else's standards might be appalling, but Henry saw nothing wrong with it. It was a business transaction, as far as he was concerned. If it turned out he would have to make a few trips to the stubborn ones, then he would do so, but that was it. His very first call was an indication of just how far he would go to get these releases and agreements signed.

Jim Leigh had been with Catalano for over fifteen years. He was a gentle giant of a man, standing six feet four inches tall, weighing two hundred seventy-five pounds. Known as the company clown and a great entertainer, he was also a top producer for the firm, and loved by all. Jimmy always dressed sloppily and routinely looked like he brushed his hair with a "pork chop." All of this seemed to make him that much more endearing to his co-workers, and more importantly, his clients. He left behind a wife, Jill, and two children; Leo (8) and Vernon (4). Henry wanted to call his widow first. He figured this guy was so well loved it would be a big advantage to have this family on his side. When he called, it was Jill who answered the phone. They exchanged pleasantries, after which Henry wasted no time going to work. He told Jill how beloved her husband was at work and how many times he had made Henry laugh. The truth was, he barely spoke to Jimmy and always felt he was a goof who had no business on Wall Street. Still, he told Jill she was the first widow he had contacted, because "Jim deserved to be the first." He was piling it on. When he heard Jill whimpering, he knew he had her right where he wanted her, and he went in for the kill.

"Jill, we want to do the right thing for everyone. It's been very hard. There are so many families…" Henry paused, not forgetting what Tom O'Brien had taught him. "Jill, we are offering the partners $100,000 above and beyond their bonuses. Also, we're going to supply seven years of medical coverage for you and the kids. And because all the remaining partners and I want to do the right thing, 50% of all profits over that seven year period will go to you and the other families." Phew! It felt good to be able to say that. "You know, Jill, the board worked very hard and a lot of sacrifices were made to be able to do this, but we all felt it was the right thing to do. No, it was the only thing to do!"

Jill was overjoyed at first, and sobbed outwardly at all the seemingly wonderful things Henry had to say about her husband. She had never even met Henry, yet he seemed to understand her husband's and her situation so well. She truly believed this offering was from the heart. However, she didn't completely buckle under right away. She maintained enough composure to ask Henry a question or two.

"How would we be paid in the future, and why is it a good idea to relinquish Jim's partnership, Henry?"

Henry had to do a little more dancing. "Jill," he paused, "I'm afraid with all the people we've lost, there is not going to be any substantial profits in the future. That's why we're giving you the $100,000 up front. We feel you could receive as much as another $100,000 over the next few years, but realistically, we simply don't have the manpower or relationships to maintain our business. I mean, how could we replace someone like Jimmy? The partnerships will be worth little or nothing in a short period of time."

Jill was hesitant to say, "yes" right away, so Henry pressed on.

"If everyone doesn't agree, we can't do this, Jill. That means virtually nothing for the hundreds of families, most of which are much less fortunate than you; some of these families have nothing right now. You see, Jill, we're all counting on each other now. It's all we have left: each other. What do you think Jimmy would do?"

Was this great stuff, or what? Henry went from game show host, "Here's what's behind door number two" to Billy Graham's "Am I not my brother's keeper?" all in one speech. It was pure poetry, and of course it worked. After just a minute of reflection, Jill caved in.

"Okay, Henry, we want to do what's best for everyone. That is the way Jimmy would want it. If you say this is the best, then I guess it is the best."

Jill could not see Henry at the other end of the phone, pumping his fist in victory. "Thank you, Jill, and God bless you."

Henry had landed his first victim—one he would use to land many more over the next few weeks. Henry's ace-in-the-hole was laying guilt on these poor widows and widowers, always dropping the other victims and their families right into their laps. He would say or do whatever it took to close the deal and get those agreements signed.

Amazingly enough, by the end of a week Henry had agreements with almost 90% of the employees on his list. As he prepared to meet with Len and Rick, he first privately met with Jim Swimhammer. Swimhammer had spent the last week fielding calls from family members, the press, and even insurance companies. Jim was never a people person, and virtually knew none of the employees personally, so, his job was putting out any little brush fires that came the company's way over that period of time. Whenever any questions came up regarding Henry, Jim went with his standard answer: "Mr. Larson is totally focusing on taking care of the families right now and not doing any interviews. He feels he must be where he is needed most." He said this with more and more conviction each time, as if he was starting to believe it himself. He had very little to report to Henry, as everything was well under control.

"How's Mr. Stevens doing, Jim?" Henry was referring, of course, to his brother Glen.

"I wish I had his life, Henry. The house he rented is beautiful. We got him this motorcycle with a…"

Henry interjected. "Why the hell are you buying him a motorcycle? I told you to get him the best. That goes for a car as well."

"Can't do that, Henry."

"Why not?"

"You see motorcycles in Bermuda don't require a drivers license. Hell, you can get one at fifteen! We haven't been able to get him a license yet. That's a lot harder than the passport, believe it or not."

Henry paused, "...all right. What else, Jim?"

"Nothing. He's got girlfriends, gets a daily massage, and plays golf. Like I said, I wish I had his life."

"That's a relief. The next time you speak to him, tell him I asked about him."

Jim nodded, as to assure Henry he would do so, as Henry continued. "Oh, by the way, I have good news for you. Now that we are close to buying out the partners, it will only be a short period of time before Catalano Securities will cease to exist. I give it two years, tops!"

"This is good news for me?"

"Not so fast, Jim; let me finish. I want you to resign and come to work exclusively for Rapid Trading."

Jim sat silently, waiting for a moment as he waited for the other shoe to drop. "And?" Jim responded.

"And, Jim, I'm making you senior advisor of Rapid Trading, with an annual salary of $500,000! I promised you would be taken care of, didn't I?"

"Yes, you did, Henry, except until now I had some doubts."

"Doubts? When have I ever not lived up to my word with you, Jim?"

While thrilled by the news, Jim couldn't help but wonder what Henry had up his sleeve. Henry never gave out anything that freely. Although Jim did have something on Henry, no one else ever had before. Perhaps Henry was paying off Jim before he asked for it himself. This, to Henry, would be acceptable, as opposed to being blackmailed which, would not. Jim shook Henry's hand and graciously accepted the job.

"Should I be in this upcoming meeting you have with Rick and Len?"

"Jim, from now on you're in every meeting."

The two men walked down the hall to the conference room where Len and Rick were waiting for them. Len and Rick handed Henry a report, showing that almost 75% of the list of employees were on board. They received very little resistance and felt they would be very close to finishing within Henry's imposed three-week period. Some of the holdouts simply weren't ready to talk yet, but Rick and Len felt that over time they would get them. Henry, of course, couldn't resist boasting how he nailed down 90% of the list by himself. Still, he was happy at the results both Len and Rick had achieved. After brief congratulations, Henry shared some insights on how he wanted Len and Rick to pressure the remaining unsigned families.

"When you go back, make sure they realize that they are keeping everyone from being paid. Make sure they realize that we owe the families an update. Do they really want the other 80% who want this to happen to know who is holding up their kids' Christmas presents?"

Nobody could turn up the heat better than Henry.

He continued, "Also, the government won't make any offers to the families until they know their final financial status. So…they're holding that up too. Put it all out there, boys; make it perfectly clear. I want those names on these agreements by November 8th!"

Henry desperately wanted to be able to present the families their money for the holidays. This, of course, was perceived as a good public relations move. Tom O'Brien even suggested sending a small news crew to accompany Henry to one or two of the more struggling families to present the gifts in person. It was a great public relation maneuver. Here's "Santa Henry" bringing turkeys and checks, delivering them to needy families just in the nick of time. The papers ate it up. Henry was almost as popular with the public as Mayor Giuliani was. Henry knew that he wouldn't get everyone by November 8th, but as long as he had 90% or better, he was going ahead with the plan. After that he would put as much pressure on the remaining families as possible. If that didn't work, he'd offer them more money. Either way, he felt sure by year's end it would be complete, and he would own all of the company's shares. As it turned out, he was right. The last holdout that, ironically, was Emily Macanee, wife of the rebellious Eddie Macanee, signed December 30th. It cost Henry an extra 200 grand, but it was worth it, as he was that much closer to his billion-dollar payoff.

# CHAPTER 12

▼

# "THE NEW YEAR"

The entire country was happy to say goodbye to the year 2001. It was a year filled with bad economy, the September 11th tragedy, and finally an attempt to infest the US with Anthrax. Hope was that 2002 would give everyone a chance to turn the page on his or her lives, but certainly 2001 would not be forgotten for a long, long time. Henry, too, was glad to usher in the New Year. After all, this would certainly be his big pay-off year. With Glen happily tucked away in Bermuda and Jim Swimhammer having resigned over his shares to take on his new job at Rapid Trading, it left only two outstanding remaining shareholders of Catalano Securities: Rick Stein and Len Abraham. Henry was certain that getting their shares would be a breeze, although he knew he couldn't insult them. They knew a lot, but neither had any idea about the impending insurance claim coming,—one worth probably twenty five million dollars apiece to them, if they kept their shares. So Henry would have to dangle a carrot in front of them—one large enough for them to accept without any hesitation. First, he had to continue feeding his good guy image. Customers had slowly and reluctantly begun doing business with Rapid Trading. They were waiting to see if Henry would follow through on his promise of taking care of his former employees' families. As December 31st represented the end of the fiscal year, Henry would have to show them he was not just blowing smoke. He would have to follow his plan as promised. The company itself made a modest profit, after paying out employees, of five million dollars. Normally Henry would reinvest that so as not to show profits for partners, but not this time. He took that sum and instructed the accountants to post fifteen of the twenty-five million he had kept from the bonus pool as profits. He made sure every news network and newspaper was made aware of it. He held a press conference, which was covered by every network, where he gleefully boasted that his company's profits of twenty million would translate into ten million to the families. When one inquiring reporter asked how Rapid Trading was doing, Henry set him straight right in front of the whole world.

"Rapid Trading is doing okay, but it has nothing to do with Catalano; that is a separate company, so let's focus on Catalano."

There, he'd said it and no one asked again. No one caught on that what Henry was really saying—what no one could see through—was his deep dark plan of deception. All of this was simply a plan to get business for Rapid Trading, something the families would never get a cent from. And now, the bait was taken. Families got checks, but they were checks they should have received months earlier as part of their bonus pool. Henry not only got his good publicity, he kept his clients happy as well.

From that point on, business at Rapid Trading started to pick up. Henry had enough money left for two or three more dog-and-pony shows before it would run out. By then he figured any problems would easily be smoothed over. No one could ever accuse him of wrong doing after all the apparent good he had done. How could they? All Henry had to do now was acquire Len Abraham's and Rick Stein's shares and the entire billion dollar insurance claim was his. This, of course, would not be considered profits, as it was an insurance settlement, therefore it belonged to the shareholders or Henry, and not to the families who had relinquished their shares in the company.

Henry invited Len and Rick to dinner to celebrate and thank them for their good work in acquiring all those partnership shares. This would be his forum. He'd lure them to a fancy dinner, wine and dine them, offer them a chance of a lifetime, then fuck them out of millions, all in a night's work.

It was the end of January 2002 and Len was due back in Tokyo in just a few days, so Henry had to move quickly. He set up the dinner at the Quilted Giraffe, a swank Manhattan dining experience. They drank $500 bottles of wine and feasted on caviar and duck. Henry toasted them several times during dinner. Afterwards, he passed around some fine Cuban cigars that Glen had given him while in Bermuda. These were a favorite of both Rick and Len. Henry knew just how to push their buttons. By the time he had them relaxed and had patted them on the back enough, he went in for the kill.

"Boys, it's time for the payback. Time to show you just how much I truly value your work. We all know Catalano is Wall Street's Titanic. It is going down, and nothing can stop it. And where does that leave you guys? With stock worth nothing! I thought about selling, but there really are no buyers right now. It's just a matter of time before it sinks."

Len peered up at Henry. He was trying to figure out just what his boss was up to. "I'm offering you both a chance to swap Catalano stock for Rapid Trading stock, even up!"

Both men took a moment, while looking at each other. They puffed on their cigars and sat back in their chairs silently, while glaring at Henry. "What the hell was he up to?" they wondered. Rick was the first to speak up.

"Is that legal, Henry?"

"Well, it's a little complicated, Rick. We would structure it the same way I did with Jim Swimhammer. You both resign your positions and stock shares at Catalano, then I hire both of you at Rapid Trading for the same salary in the same position, with the same amount of stock you had at Catalano."

Len rubbed his chin, puffed on his cigar, then took a deep breath, while exhaling a large cloud of smoke. "What about Catalano?"

"You both agree to stay on for six months as consultants. By then I'll either sell what's left of it or it will be worthless. If I sell, we'll give the families 50% of all the profits, as promised but I don't see that being much."

"Henry, you promised them insurance for seven years!"

"No, Rick, I said we'd use company profits to pay that. If I sell it, they should all recover enough money to buy insurance for those years and more! What else can I do?"

Henry seemed a little annoyed at Rick's constant challenges.

"Why is it, Rick, every time I try to do something good you bring sarcasm or cynicism into it? Why can't you just say 'thank you'?"

Len and Rick knew that this was, in fact, a very generous offer. Nothing they could say would change his mind or his opinions. They could either take it or go down with the ship. As Henry predicted, they took it. Catalano's fate was now sealed, and Henry's billion dollars was all but in the bank. Henry had the agreements drawn up the next morning so Len could sign it before he headed back to Tokyo. He didn't want to take any chances that either one of them might change their minds. They all agreed to keep this quiet so as not to trigger a mass exodus before Henry could dump what was left of the company.

After Len and Rick signed over their shares, Henry began filing his insurance claim. The beauty was that no one had to be told about it, as there were no stockholders left except Henry, and of course Glen, but he was presumed dead with no heir to his shares. By agreement, his shares went back to the company—or Henry. It would take several months for the claim to be paid, so Henry celebrated by going to see his brother.

Through Jim, they agreed that Henry would fly to Bermuda this time. He took a one-day trip early in February and Glen met him later that evening. Once again, they made sure it was under the utmost secrecy. Henry rented a boat and they left from a secluded dockyard on the end of the island. Henry greeted Glen with several hugs.

"Man, I miss you."

Glen whispered as they toasted their apparent success. Glen seemed a bit depressed, but truly delighted to see his brother.

"Jim tells me things are good here, Glen."

"Yeah, I guess…"

"You guess? What does that mean? I saw the house, and he tells me you're certainly not lonely."

They both smiled, but Glen stopped abruptly. "Yeah, that's good and all, but…"

"But what?" Henry snapped.

Glen paused. He looked at his brother like a kid about to tell his parents he'd broken their most precious vase while playing ball. He sighed and thought, what the hell, here it goes.

"I'll tell you what, Henry. How long can you be on vacation, Henry, huh? I kind of miss home. I had to spend the holidays alone. I didn't even so much as have a dog to say Merry Christmas to. I couldn't even call the only family I have left: you, Kate, little Henry, Courtney…I couldn't even tell them Merry Christmas. You know what I did, Henry?"

Henry stayed silent.

"I got myself drunk for Christmas, passed out about two in the afternoon and woke up the next morning. That's how I got through it, Henry. All my relationships come and go in a couple of weeks. Everybody else goes back to reality except me."

Henry paused for just a minute while he thought.

"I'm sorry about Christmas, Glen. Kate cried for you. It was sad for me, too. It killed me to let her continue to believe you're dead. It'll get better, bro, I promise. I'll get you a dog…"

Glen blurted out, "It's not about the fuckin' dog, Henry!"

Henry tried to calm him down. "Okay Glen, okay! We'll move you to another island."

"For how long, Henry? How long before it becomes the same routine?"

"Well, Glen, do you want to go to London? Australia? You name it!"

Glen took a long pause, looked at his brother and spoke the words Henry dreaded hearing. "Home, Henry—the States. I want to go home."

Henry's stomach began to churn. This was something he had not expected, nor did he have a response for his brother. He took a deep breath, slowly exhaled, with a hint of a sigh. Finally Henry's dander got up a bit and he went at Glen.

"Jesus, Glen, we had an agreement. I gave you twenty-five million dollars. I set you up with a life people would die for..." a bad pun on Henry's part, "...and now you want to do this. Do you realize how this could affect me? Do you even care?"

Glen knew Henry's ability to spin a situation and put guilt everywhere but on himself. This time he fought back.

"You gave me nothing! You paid me off so you wouldn't look like a liar. You were afraid that people would find out you knew about the attack. That money is blood money for all those people who died that day. Besides, you forget that I know about the insurance money, and twenty-five million wouldn't be a good tip on what you're making on it, so don't preach to me. I'm not complaining, but with all that money can't you find a way to bring me back?"

After arguing for the better part of the night, Henry realized he was not going to change his brother's mind, at least not at that time. The insurance was due within a month or two, and he needed to buy some time.

"Okay, Glen, okay. Maybe you're right. Maybe I'm being too paranoid. Besides, it doesn't have to be New York, right?"

"No, Henry; California, Chicago, just some place with a lot of people where I can start a life, where people don't come and go on a weekly basis."

"Okay, Glen, okay, but you have to give me some time. Let me talk to Jim and see what we can come up with."

Glen looked relieved, to say the least. "Great, Henry! I knew you'd understand. I mean, you are all the family and friends I have left in the world. So talk to Jim, work it out. I'll wait for you, just not too long. I can't take too much more." Henry nodded and hugged his brother. For the next few hours the brothers drank, but did very little talking.

A little while later the boat was back on the dock and Henry was on his way back home. It was the longest two-hour flight back to New York of his life. Everything had been going as planned. The last thing he expected was this: his brother fucking up his plans. But maybe Glen was right. Maybe there was a way to do this without ruining everything. Perhaps enough time had passed where people wouldn't even ask. He's only one person. Surely Henry, with all his connections and financial wealth, could pull this off.

Henry's plane landed at 11:00 p.m. in Newark. The minute he stepped off the plane, he called Jim Swimhammer. Jim was sleeping at home when the call came.

"Jim, it's Henry. I need you. I need to meet with you right away."

"Tonight, Henry?"

"That's what right away is, right, Jim?"

Jim recognized Henry's sarcasm. This was a sign that Henry was not going to wait, so suggesting they meet in the morning was out of the question.

"Okay, where?"

"I'll get a room at the Newark Airport Marriott under your name. Call from the lobby when you get here."

Jim made the thirty-minute trip to the Marriott, arriving just before midnight. After calling Henry, he went to room 827, where Henry was nervously waiting. He told Jim he wanted to bring Glen back to the States.

"I miss him, Jim, and besides, who's going to know who he is? We'll put him in L.A. or Chicago. I mean, it's not like someone's looking for him. What would the problem be?"

Jim looked directly at Henry, while keeping silent. First he wanted to see if he was serious. When he realized that he was, he walked to the window and looked out of it. A moment later he spun around, facing Henry.

"Are you out of your fucking mind, Henry? You want us both to sink here? No one is looking for him? Are your for real? He's lonely, getting all those massages, playing golf, getting laid? Boo-fucking-hoo for him. So he wants to come back, get a job, huh? How about if someone does a background check on him? They might find it interesting to discover that he's dead! What story do you go with then, huh? This is political suicide. Every government agency will investigate you and everyone close to you. You can't do this, Henry, and I think you know it."

Indeed Henry did. He just needed to hear it from Jim. He had to be sure he wasn't being paranoid, that his fears were real, and that Glen, in reality, couldn't come back. He told Jim about their conversation in Bermuda. He explained how desperate Glen sounded and his fear that Glen may try to come back—with or without Henry's permission.

"What the hell do we do, Jim? This is my brother. How do we handle this?"

"I don't know, Henry. How much time do we have?"

"Maybe a month, two on the outside, that's it."

"Okay, I'll think of something. Give me a couple of days. Now, if there's nothing else, I'm tired and would like to go back home, unless you have another bomb to drop on me."

"No, that's it, Jim."

Henry waited for Jim to leave. He poured himself a drink from the room's mini-bar, replaying the words Glen had spoken to him just a few hours ago. Then, about ten minutes later, he left the hotel and went home.

The following week, Henry and Jim sat down in Henry's office. Jim closed the door and sat across from Henry.

"Henry, I've assessed the situation. You need to understand everything at stake. Glen Larson died September 11th. He doesn't exist anymore. We can't bring him back to life. Catalano Securities is all but history. Rapid Trading is on schedule to gross over two hundred million dollars if it continues on the pace it's going. Our overhead in the company is less than forty million. That makes our profit margin 80%. Eighty fucking percent, Henry! I don't have to tell you what that means. Catalano, in its best year, never posted so much as a 40% profit margin. Now I don't have to tell you how much money that means for the company and it's shareholders. Let's add to the mix that if Glen somehow rises from the dead, people may sniff around and uncover that insurance policy you're about to cash in on. What do you think happens then? I guess what I'm saying, Henry, is that Glen died tragically on September 11th. And as tragic as that is, he needs to stay dead. If he comes back to the States, even under a different name, it would be a disaster. He couldn't get a job under his new name because he'd have no traceable background unless he came back as Glen Larson. We've already gone over what that means. So you need to make him understand this. Remind him about the money. Tell him that if he comes back he loses the money. Maybe that will shake him. Do whatever it takes. There are a lot of places he can go. We can send him anywhere in the world, but not here!"

Henry glared at Jim, while nodding his head up and down. Jim was right about everything and he knew it, but now Henry had the dreaded job of having to strong-arm his own brother. Still, it had to be done. Jim and Henry agreed to wait until the insurance money was paid before giving Glen the bad news. Jim would contact Glen and string him along under the premise that they were close to bringing him back. It was the only way to keep Glen from doing something drastic, like showing up in the States and jeopardizing Henry's payday. Jim did just that. Over the next month he fed Glen just enough information to make him feel that they were close to a solution.

# CHAPTER 13

▼

# CHECKMATE FOR
# HENRY

It was the 16$^{th}$ of April when a courier arrived at the door of Rapid Trading. He brought the pot of gold Henry had been waiting for: a check for just under one billion dollars. During the previous month Henry had been busy unloading what was left of Catalano Securities. He found an overseas buyer who was willing to pay him thirty-five million dollars for a company only eight months earlier that had been worth twenty times that, but Henry didn't care. He would be able to close the chapter on Catalano and all the families from September 11$^{th}$. He would have his own company that was three times as profitable as Catalano with less than one-tenth of the partners. Besides, he could still walk away with seventeen million dollars from the sale, along with the billion dollars he'd received from the insurance company. What could be better? He would take the other eighteen million and divide it among the families. He could package that with the ten million left from the employees' bonus pool, making twenty eight million. He planned to put that money in an annuity that would cover insurance premiums for five years on the families. After that, each family would receive a lump sum pay out of about $50,000 each. Henry's commitment to them would be paid in full, at least in his mind. Henry felt that would put him in good standing with the families and his clients. Since they didn't know about the billion-dollar insurance policy, they would think he was a stand-up guy. His public image would never be greater. He was once again the subject of every talk show host, all of them praising his efforts to salvage a dying company and doing what was best for his lost employees and their families. All he had left to do was solve the riddle of his brother.

On Monday, April 28th, once again Henry boarded a plane to Bermuda. He made his way down to the dockyard and met Glen in a local tavern. The news brought, however, was not what Glen was expecting. Over the last few months Jim had been filling Glen's head with visions of him coming back to the States. When Jim told him Henry was coming, he began packing, thinking his brother was coming to take him home. When Henry started talking about him not coming back, Glen reacted as if he had just been stabbed in the back.

"All these months, Henry, you've been stringing me along?"

"It's not like that, Glen. We've been trying to figure out a way. It's just impossible right now. Maybe in a year or two."

"A year or two…what am I, stupid? How many times do you think I'll fall for the same bullshit, Henry? You can't find a way! My brother, the billionaire, can't find a way to do something for his little brother!"

"Well, then I'll find a way."

Henry could see that Glen's resolve had only become stronger over the last few months. He had one more card up his sleeve, and it was time to play it.

"All right, Glen, I'll make you a deal. You stay here or go anywhere else other than the States and I'll give you another twenty-five million dollars. But if you insist on coming back, you get nothing. That means giving back the twenty-five million I gave you!"

Henry was sure Glen might reconsider with this generous offer—or threat—but Glen did not. Over the past four months, Glen's twenty-five million had accrued a little under one million dollars in interest, so even by giving Henry back his money, Glen could come back home with just under a million dollars. Glen laughed, but quickly his grin turned to a smirk.

"You think life's all about money, Henry, don't you?" Maybe I felt that way, too, but the last six months gave me the opportunity to see things differently. I don't care about the fucking money any more. See, I actually miss you and Kate and the kids. I feel guilty everyday about what happened that day. I see my friends, Tom and Louie, in my sleep, and how I just left them there. No warning, nothing. I could have sent them somewhere, done something, but no, I couldn't jeopardize your precious plan. So now they're gone. Fuck the money! I choose coming home." Although shocked by Glen's decision, Henry knew the game was over. He was out of ideas. He stared at Glen, while reflecting on Glen's words. He understood what his brother was saying; he just didn't see it his way.

"Are you sure, Glen, that there's nothing I can do or say to change your mind?"

"Did you listen to anything I said, Henry?"

"I love you—you're my brother—but this is no life for me. I promise I'll stay away from New York, but please understand, this is not about you." Henry sighed before answering Glen.

"Still, Glen, will you do me one favor?"

"What is it, Henry?"

"If we do this, bring you back I mean, it has to be on my terms. We have to be able to put you somewhere safe, somewhere where people don't know you. You can't just show up at Yankee Stadium for a ball game. If we have to bring you back, you have to respect whatever way we do it. Is that fair?"

"Very fair, Henry. Just tell me where and when."

"Let me finish, Glen. I want you to please—reconsider this decision. Tomorrow when I get to my office I'll check my overseas accounts. If nothing has changed, I'll transfer you twenty-five million more and we'll talk about where we can send you outside the U.S. Remember, Glen, that's anywhere...Rio, Italy, Bora Bora, you name it. I'm sure there are places you would truly be happy if you just gave them a chance. Think about it, for me." Henry paused and Glen spoke.

"And if I still want to come back?"

"Well, if you still insist, when I access my account if I see twenty-five million dollars transferred to my account I'll send Jim over to take you back. If that happens, remember you agreed we do this on my terms and you agree to go wherever I send you."

Henry gave Glen that puppy-dog look, while staring into his eyes and put his hands on both shoulders. Glen had seen this before. He looked down, away from his brother, as if to say "no."

"Either way, Glen, we keep communications the same. Don't call me. I'll have Jim call you."

"Thanks, Henry, but that money will be there by 9:00 a.m. Go tell Jim to start packing. I want to come home by Wednesday."

"Well, I'll wait 'til morning, just in case you change your mind. Twenty-five million is a lot of dough. It's several lifetimes of happiness. Think, Glen, think."

He hugged Glen for what seemed to be several minutes, and then made his way back to the airport.

This time, when his plane landed in Newark, Jim Swimhammer was waiting for him. Jim took one look at Henry and knew.

"I guess I'm going to Bermuda, huh?"

"Guess so, Jim. He wants to be home by Wednesday."

"Jesus, Henry, today is Monday. Does he think we're magicians? I have to get passports, make reservations, and figure out where to send him—in twenty-four hours! That's fucking ridiculous! I'm not a fucking travel agent, Henry. These things take time, certainly more than a day."

"Jim, if you don't go, he won't wait. Somehow you have to make it happen. If anyone can take care of this, you can."

After a sign of frustration, Jim nodded, and they went their separate ways. When Henry got home, he went directly in to take a shower, and then locked himself in his office, once again shutting everyone out, including his wife Kate. He drank scotch after scotch until about 2:00 am, when he passed out on the couch in his den.

The next morning Henry deliberately arrived at work late. He strolled into his office at 10:00 am and slowly accessed his accounts on his computer. After a few minutes he reluctantly called up his overseas account last. As he feared, there it was. Just as Glen promised, twenty-five million dollars had been transferred. Both accounts were drawn out of Switzerland, and they went by numbers, not names, so they were difficult to trace. Henry set up accounts this way so he could send Glen money without anyone knowing whom it went to or where it came from. He called Jim, who was waiting at Newark airport for the noon flight to Bermuda.

"The money is there, Jim. I guess he is willing to come home a pauper rather than live like a king." Henry said this; having no idea about the additional million Glen had saved. Glen never told him.

Jim boarded the plane and was on his way to Bermuda. Glen, meanwhile, was busy getting ready. He had packed what clothes he had and was anxiously awaiting Jim's arrival. When Jim arrived at Glen's house, just after 4:00 p.m., he greeted him with a handshake and a hug.

"What took you so long, Jim? I thought Henry changed his mind."

"Nah, customs likes breaking balls 'cause I had no luggage." He then handed Glen a ticket to Chicago with the name "Thomas Sean Lynch" on it.

"What's this, Jim?"

"Can't use your name, Glen, and after today Brian Stevens won't exist. Here you go." He gave Glen a new passport with his picture and his new name, Thomas Lynch. "Remember, Glen, you agreed to do it whatever way Henry wanted."

"It's okay with me, Jim, I just don't know why we have to change my name again. I was just getting used to being Brian Stevens."

"Well, Glen, he's your brother and you know how paranoid he is." After a second pause, they both laughed. "Our flight is at 7:00 a.m., so we need to be out of here by 4:30 a.m. That's not too early is it?"

"Shit, Jim, I'm ready now. I don't think I'll even sleep a wink tonight."

Jim opened a brown paper bag he had brought with him. This one contained two bottles of Jack Daniels. "I picked these up on the way over here. I thought it might help."

Glen smiled and got them a few glasses and some ice. Several hours later both bottles were empty. Glen chattered away to Jim about all his plans once he got back to the sStates.

"Pizza! The first thing I'm going to get is a pizza. Between Florida and here, I haven't had a good slice of pizza in six months." He continued on about going to ball games and seeing snow. "Anything but a beach!"

When both bottles were empty, Glen had done most of the damage. It seemed like Jim was acting like a designated-pourer. By 1:00 a.m. Glen faded, falling asleep on the couch. Jim tossed a blanket on him. "Now you'll sleep good, Glen." Then he retired to the spare bedroom.

At about 4:00 a.m. the next morning, Jim woke Glen up. Glen was still very hung over from the night before.

"It's time, Glen. Let's get moving."

Glen slowly dragged himself off the couch, still smarting from the night before. Meanwhile, Jim wandered out the back door, admiring the view from the terrace. "I can't believe you're giving all this up. It's so quiet and peaceful, no one around to bother you. I told your brother I'd gladly switch places with you."

Glen wearily wandered over to Jim, taking in the view for the last time. He noticed that Jim had conveniently set his bags by the door. He couldn't believe he was actually going home. He had a splitting headache, but he didn't care; he was too excited about leaving.

"What's in Chicago, Jim? Why did you pick there?"

"I don't know, Glen. It's just away from the whole Wall Street thing, you know. I figured if we put you somewhere no one from 'the Street' really goes, Henry will feel more at ease. We're working on finding you a job, but that's gonna take a little more work on our part, especially since we don't have a social security number for you yet, but be patient. I'll get it done."

By now Glen wasn't concerned about any of that. He simply wanted to touch down back in the U.S. He walked toward Jim, who was still glaring at the beautiful beach and ocean that lay directly below them.

"It's a beautiful view, but after a while it gets lonely looking at it by yourself, Jim. Can you understand that?"

Glen rubbed his eyes, trying to wake up enough to take one last look at the view Jim was so jealous of, but at that exact moment Jim lunged at him. He grabbed Glen by the shoulders of his shirt, and within a second threw Glen over the railing overlooking the water. Glen toppled down the steep cliff, banging along the rocky mountainside several times before his body made it all the way down the 200 feet and he splashed into the ocean. Glen never made a sound. As Jim looked down, he could barely see Glen's body floating in the dark water. He waited a few minutes to make sure the body wasn't moving. Then Jim finished the job. He calmly went back into the house and unpacked Glen's bags. He put everything back in its place. He cleaned and put away his glass, sitting next to the two empty bottles of scotch, giving the appearance that Glen had drunk both bottles himself. Jim then took the airline ticket and passport he had given Glen with Thomas Lynch's name on them. Jim was out of the door by 5:00 a.m. and on his way to deliver the bad news to Henry, who was nervously waiting in his office. It would be several hours, Jim figured, before Glen's body would be recovered. An inspection of his apartment would turn up no clues. It would appear that Glen, or Brian Stevens, after drinking two bottles of Jack Daniels must have stumbled and fallen over the railing. It would be ruled an accident. Since there was no other information on Brian Stevens, the case would be closed. Of course Jim knew all of this before he sent Glen plunging down to certain death.

At about noon Jim arrived at Henry's office and delivered the bad news. Henry broke down crying for several minutes before pulling himself back together. He paced his office, while reminiscing about his brother.

"He was a good kid, Jim."

"I know, Henry."

"No, you don't. When we were kids he would follow me around everywhere, always trying to imitate me. He would do anything for me." Then Henry paused, looking out his office window. "I guess he really did die on September 11th, just like the rest of them." Henry rubbed his eyes and once again looked toward Jim.

"I transferred the money Glen sent back to me over to your account as agreed—twenty-five million dollars, Jim. For that, I don't ever want to discuss this again. I never want to hear Glen's name mentioned by you again. Understand?"

Jim shook his head, acknowledging, "yes" to Henry, although he wasn't sure of Henry's motive. Was it because Jim had killed his brother, or maybe Henry had to pay twenty-five million dollars to put away the only other person, besides Jim Swimhammer, who could tell the world the truth? Either way, this was a perfect scenario for both Henry and Jim. Jim knew that if Henry tried to take any action against him, as he did his brother, he would have to employ an outsider, and that was too dangerous. Henry would never trust someone he had no leverage on. As for Jim, Henry now had some peace of mind as well. Jim was the only remaining living person who knew the truth—the only one who could bring him down. Yet if he did, he would go down even harder, having killed Glen. Both men were bound by their actions. This was the only true partnership Henry had to honor in his life, and so it was.

As Henry and Jim sat in his office, they pondered their next venture. They were partners now. Henry peered at the television, where he had been watching CNBC, as he did every business day. Senator Jon Corzine was speaking, and Henry was shaking his head as if he were disgusted.

"What is it, Henry?"

"This guy…he's so full of it!"

Henry turned to Jim. "You know, Jim, I've been thinking. With Catalano Securities gone and Rapid Trading rolling, maybe it's time for me to do something more with my life."

Jim had no idea where Henry was going with this, but he humored him. "Do more what?"

"Well, look at Corzine. And Bloomberg. Corzine was one of Goldman Sachs' top executives for years, while Mike Bloomberg started the most successful information system in history. Now one is a senator and the other is running for mayor of New York! I'm smarter than both of them, and right now the public loves me more than both of those guys put together."

Jim just stared and listened. Henry strolled around his office, holding a drink in his right hand.

"Think about it, Jim."

"What, Henry?"

"I have the public right where I want them. They trust me, and that's what gets people elected. Yeah, that's what's next, Jim."

Henry continued to stare at the television, but his vision was clear. Once again he raised his glass, this time to toast himself. He had a billion dollar war chest and knew just what he wanted to do with it: *Governor Henry Larson!*

The works and insightfulness of Mr. Oliver Stone inspired this book. Any similarities in names or mannerisms of anyone in this book are purely coincidental.

This book is also dedicated to the families of the friends and associates that bravely lost their lives in the name of freedom. We pray that you, and the memory of what you died for, will be forever in our minds.

Brian S. Marro

0-595-30527-X